Carlos Maleno

THE IRISH SEA

Translated from the Spanish by Eric Kurtzke

DALKEY ARCHIVE PRESS

Library of Congress Cataloging-in-Publication Data
Names: Maleno, Carlos, 1977 author. | Kurtzke, Eric.
Title: The Irish sea / by Carlos Maleno ; translated by Eric Kurtzke.
Other titles: Mar de Irlanda. English
Description: First Dalkey Archive edition. | Victoria, TX : Dalkey Archive
Press, 2017. | "Originally published in Spanish by Editorial Sloper as Mar
de Irlanda in 2014" [Palma de Mallorca]
Identifiers: LCCN 2016054357 | ISBN 9781943150144 (pbk. : alk. paper)
Subjects: | GSAFD: Fantasy fiction.
Classification: LCC PQ6713.A327 M3713 2017 | DDC 863/.7--dc23
LC record available at https://lccn.loc.gov/2016054357

GOBIERNO DE ESPAÑA

MINISTERIO
DE EMPLEO
Y SEGURIDAD SOCIAL

This work has been published with a subsidy from the Ministry of Education, Culture and Sport of Spain.

www.dalkeyarchive.com
Victoria, TX / McLean, IL / Dublin

Dalkey Archive Press publications are, in part, made possible through the support of the University of Houston-Victoria and its programs in creative writing, publishing, and translation.

Printed on permanent/durable acid-free paper

I. Far from the Irish Sea

Kafka's Successors

I AM AT a giant, boundless party, it could be the party for the end of the world, I tell myself, but it's only another party for the end of the year. Midnight strikes and I hear the faint sounds of the fireworks outside, as though in another world, making their way through the frenetic pop music. I like parties because the frenetic music hangs over everything at such high volume that all conversation becomes impossible. I like these kinds of parties because I don't have to maintain conversations that were impossible anyway. Besides, I can drink a lot more. Can, and do.

Everyone's kissing and wishing each other happy New Year, and people I don't know kiss me, as do others I barely know, which comes to the same thing. Someone hugs me, and when I look surprised, he asks if I really don't remember him, and I don't, but I say of course I remember. He says he has plenty to tell me, then vanishes and reappears smiling, like a friendly ghost from some children's story, and offers me a glass, which I take, and together we drink a toast to the new year, or perhaps to the end of the world, I'm not quite sure, and of course he has nothing to say.

He has nothing to say, but what he has instead is a woman he introduces me to. A woman with big blue eyes whose name I don't catch amid the blaring rhythms wrapped around everything, a woman who dances up to me and at first says something I can't make out, turning her back as if on purpose to some friend we have in common, whom I don't know either, and ignoring him she says something else to me, this time talking into my ear, her body pressed against mine.

"I never go to bed with a man the first time round," she says, and she's drunk.

I'm drunk, too, at least a little. At parties, I don't drink enough to forget. As long as I don't forget what happens, later at home I'll write about the rhythm of the dancing bodies, dancing and collapsing. Collapsing at the end of the night, collapsing at the edge of horror or dreams, wasted, high on cocaine, and spilling bodily fluids on others' bodies, until they get lost in themselves, or, as they believe, in someone else, to the point of forgetting, the point of vomit, the point of fitful sleep. When I'm done writing, then I do drink to forget, trying above all to forget about her, about Elena.

I also say these things to the woman who's dancing with me, just to say something, even though I know she won't hear me over the perpetual dance beat, its rhythm eternal and easy to dance to, like death. But that's why I tell her, because I know she won't hear me, just so I don't seem asocial. She presses her body closer and says:

"What? I can't hear you over the music."

I lean in and say in her ear:

"I don't go to bed with a woman the first time either, in fact, it's been a long time since I've gone to bed with any woman at all," and I think but don't say that I haven't gone to bed with anyone since Elena died.

"What?" she says again, and taking my arm she pulls me toward the door that leads to the terrace, and outside it's cold, as cold as it can be on the last night of December in the Northern Hemisphere, as cold as it can be on the final night of the world.

"I have to get my coat," I say.

"But first, tell me what you said inside," she says.

"I said it's been a good few fifths of gin since I've slept with a woman," I say.

"Then it hasn't been so long," she says, and lights a cigarette, watching me as she takes deep drags and exhales smoke that rises through her long dark hair. I leave her like this, wrapped in smoke as if she were burning, and briefly step inside, to set off in search of my coat among jostling bodies and the smell of perfume and sweat. When I come back, she's talking with the man who introduced us. As I walk up to them, he stops talking, gives me a complicit look, and, slapping me on the back, returns to the commotion inside. I look at her inquiringly, tilting my chin at the guy as he walks away and disappears through the door and into the crowd.

"Oh! He told me so much about you," she says.

"So much about me? How . . . ? You were hardly with him for two minutes."

"Two minutes? What are you talking about? I've been waiting on you for two hours. It's a good thing he came, I nearly died of exposure out here all by myself. I was just about to leave, you know, the only reason I didn't was for you."

And then a momentary vision comes to my mind, of one more glass of gin, then another, and then a white dust flying up like talcum powder being blown, and the dust being reflected in a dirty bathroom mirror, and a voice saying shit, and then the sour smell of vomit among the muted strains of a remix of an old David Bowie song.

"The only reason I didn't leave was for you," she repeats.

"For me?" I say.

"For you," she says. And adds, "He told me you already know, and he told me what you're looking for, too."

"Is that right? And what is it I know? And while you're at it, you could explain what I'm looking for, then we'll both be up to date."

"You know I'm from the planet Lux," she says.

"The planet Lux," I repeat, and add sarcastically, "like the vacuum cleaners."

"She's from the planet Lux, too," she says, ignoring my comment, "and I know you're looking for her."

"What are you talking about?" I say, raising my voice. "Are you crazy or something?"

"You're looking for Elena," she says.

"Elena's dead," I say, and once again everything's full of white dust in suspension and I'm looking at my bloodshot eyes in a mirror. I wet down my face and hair, slicking it back. I try to figure out how I could have arrived in this bathroom, when I was outside on the terrace with her. With her, who's now entering the bathroom and reaching for my hand, her big blue eyes are red, too, and she's yelling that it's the feast day of Saint Cocaine, and as she yells she points to the mirror, at the image of the big red drops dripping from my nose, and then she bursts into a fit of raucous laughter and drags me out of the bathroom, swimming through a maelstrom of dancing bodies. And then, over the giant loudspeakers, the song "Heart in a Cage" starts to play. The guitars rip through the air and deranged bodies dance to the rhythm of the drums. She drags me through arms, legs, faces, eyes, black leather jackets, and Julian Casablancas's voice singing: "I don't feel better / When I'm fucking around / And I don't write better / When I'm stuck in the ground / So don't teach me a lesson / 'Cause I've already learned / Yeah, the sun will be shining / And my children will burn." And then I fall down on the floor and someone steps then falls on top of me, and Casablancas keeps singing: "Yeah, we got left / Now it's three in the morning and you're eating alone / Oh the heart beats in its cage / All our friends, they're laughing at us / All of those you loved you mistrust / Help me, I'm just not quite myself / Look around, there's no one else left / I went to the concert / And I fought through the crowd / Guess I got too excited / When I thought you were around / I'm sorry you were thinking / I would steal your fire / The heart beats in its cage / Yes, the heart beats in its cage." And I feel as if I couldn't agree with him more.

Then I see her blue eyes looking back at me through the

crowd, her big blue eyes, seeming to call me, and think to myself that I might as well give in. So now she's pulling me away from the party altogether, out into the street, and the guitars are still echoing in my head as she stops a taxi and we climb inside, where I press myself against her body as she talks to me, leaning in very close, so close that I notice her unknown, strange breath and wonder what I'm doing here with this woman and think of Elena, but I don't want to think of her and I yell out, No! and the driver halts the taxi, but she tells him it's fine, explaining that I'm sick, and asks him to keep going, so he starts driving again until we pull up at a place which I don't remember, but which seems somehow familiar.

We get out of the cab and the streetlamps are shining like stars or exploding atomic bombs, and I understand that this comparison might not be ideal, but it's what I think. She unlocks a front door and, since there's no elevator, we take the stairs to her apartment on the third floor. We go inside and she offers me a drink, I say yes, and she opens a cocktail cabinet, pours out two glasses, and we sit down on a soft green sofa. She slips off her shoes, crosses two infinite legs, takes a long swig from her glass, and touches my face. I caress her white thighs, pushing up her skirt on the green felt, and she brings her face nearer mine and, with our faces almost touching, asks me:

"But don't you want to see her?"

"What . . . ?"

"Don't you want to see Elena?" she asks.

I feel dazed, as if I no longer understand anything, but then it dawns on me that it's all a joke, simply a cruel joke this woman is playing on me, and I can feel the anger welling up inside of me. And at the same time I feel drops of blood falling from my nose onto the sofa's green fabric, and I throw my head back, trying to stem the hemorrhaging. Then I think I could kill her right here, in her apartment. I picture myself breaking my glass over her head and think, that's it, I'm going to do it, when a door opens and Elena enters the room.

She enters the room, while next to me I also notice the smile of the woman with the big blue eyes, which turns quickly into a deranged laugh. Elena looks at me and says Javier, and then she walks over to the couch and touches my hand with her long mist-like fingers, saying:

"Javier, it's me, I've missed you terribly, I've been so far away." Then she takes my hand and leads me into another room, lit by a small lamp's weak light, and shuts the door behind her. From the other side of the door I can hear the muffled sound of the other woman's laughter. Then I don't hear anything, and Elena leads me to a bed stationed in the middle of the room, where we lie down. She kisses me softly, barely brushing my lips, and we undress each other slowly, without rushing; then again, I can tell that my experience of time and space is fairly subjective. At times, the room seems enormous, and at others it looks incredibly small. Both of us now naked, I feel her body's geometry, her warm breath, her tongue in my mouth, and her long fingers like fluttering wings turning out the light.

Winged creature of Lux / That brings dark and soothes pain / I got too excited when I thought you were around, sings Julian Casablancas in my dream just before I awake, in the middle of the night, to a darkness as complete as if it were the final darkness, or which perhaps is, in which case I must be dead. I try to remember where the lamp had been, my memory doesn't betray me and I find it. I turn on the dim light and look at the sleeping, naked body of the woman on the bed. I search for my coat among the clothes strewn across the floor, find it, and take my small notebook from one of the pockets. And I write. I write to give order to everything in my head. I write about this farce. About this enormous farce, here, in the faint glow of this night light, beside the sleeping body of this woman who says she's Elena, but who clearly isn't, and doesn't even look like her. I write these things down while tears flow down my face, falling on the notebook and blurring the lines of blue ink.

"Why are you crying?" Elena then asks me, the real Elena. I look at her, lifting my head from the desk. "Are you all right, Javier? You just started crying out of nowhere while you were writing," she says.

The bright daylight, filtered through the curtains, is palpable behind the living room windows of our home, here in Reykjavík. And Elena comes over and sits down on my knees and I can feel the weight of her slight body, as if it were real, or at least more real than anything else surrounding me: the objects, the walls, and beyond them: the city, the sea, the endless light of the Arctic summer, so distant from the terminal darkness of the end of the world. Then she brings her lips to mine and kisses me.

"And in that moment the man said to himself / What I wouldn't give for the joy / Of being at your side in Iceland / Under the great unmoving day / And sharing the present / Like one shares music / Or the taste of fruit. / And in that precise moment / The man was with her in Iceland," Borges once wrote.

"Borges was the thought that Kafka didn't write down, when he realized he was going to die," I say to Elena, who looks at me, puzzled, "and, in a similar way, we don't exist either," I continue, "we're only part of something written. Something written by a man who, even though he's also named Javier, is someone else. We're part of his story, of his imagination, of his efforts to order a reality he doesn't understand. We're part of an invention he made to deny that his wife, who he thinks is dead, and who, even though she's named Elena, isn't you, but at the same time is, has come back from the far-off planet Lux to be with him. We're part of his story, as he writes it, desperately, at the side of his wife as she sleeps, exhausted after a night of love and her nearly endless voyage from the limits of the universe. But the story that Javier is writing is, in turn, part of another story, which is, likewise, part of an infinite chain. Literature is always an expedition in search of truth. We approach truth, we try to fence it off, we write, giving order on paper to our ideas, to ourselves, and as a result we exist. We approach truth through someone who writes, but who's moving just as we are on a genuinely endless voyage, since truth is literature itself, both the end and the means, which is perpetually moving and we, poor unfortunates, can only hope to be Kafka's insignificant, humble successors."

Lucubration on the Aesthetics
of a Dead Man's Ethics

WHY AM I wearing on my face, at this moment, the mask of an aged Felipe González? Out of political commitment? No, I feel no political affinity with anyone, not anymore. Let's imagine that our politician, or any other politician, has a dog, which he never takes for a walk. Absolutely never. What does it matter to the dog whether this politician belongs to the left or the right?

I'm that dog.

Metaphorically speaking (of course).

I don't go for walks now either because I'm sick, very sick, not to mention the mask of Felipe González I'm wearing. But I have now neither time nor courage to explain why I'm wearing it, because at the moment I have more important things to do. Things that require my full attention.

Like dying.

Like making the last phone call of my life before I die. Like calling, as I've done on countless occasions, the magnificent medium Walter Solo. So I call him, gathering my last strength to grip this filthy phone I've requested from this no less filthy hospital as one of my two last wishes. The other is to be buried wearing the mask of Felipe González, so that if she is there, she can recognize me. This is what I must do: be Felipe González, on the other side, in whatever begins when everything ends. On the other end of the line I hear the labored breathing, like so many times before, of the renowned Walter Solo. And I hear his familiar voice, serious, monotone, on the other end, asking me what it is I wish to know. I ask about her, and as ever an

11

endless silence is his only answer. An endless silence in which all that can be heard is his labored breathing. Then I ask him about himself, ask where he is, out of the blue, in order to catch him by surprise, because I know that she's with him.

"Where are you?" I ask.

"In the beyond."

"Beyond where?"

Then the line cuts out and with it the voice of the medium Walter Solo, as well as my last hope of knowing where he is. And my time is up, I die. I die, and my dying is like anyone else's, without a tunnel of light, without a few last words, without any of those things. Without any of those things and more alone than a dog. A dog whose master, a politician by profession, never takes him for walks.

I die. Let me revel in this small sentence, since there are so few occasions to say it: one in life and none in death.

I die.

I die and they call someone, a relative or someone who claims to be my friend. And they place me in a beautiful oak coffin and bury me with my mask, respecting my final wish, and with a book, too, by Philip Roth. And I wonder how they haven't realized that I never liked Roth, how they didn't realize it was only a pose. They don't even bury me with one of Roth's masterpieces, like *American Pastoral*, or *Portnoy's Complaint*, or *The Human Stain*, but with a minor work like *The Professor of Desire*. At least this selection might redeem whoever introduced a book by Philip Roth into my coffin, my new home, my mint-condition, oaken vehicle, like a Rolls Royce en route to eternal life. Because the fact is, if there's any Philip Roth character with whom I could identify, it would have to be with the protagonist of *The Professor of Desire*, and if there's anything that's dominated the last years of my life it's been that: desire.

Desire for Her.

And now that I'm dead and at rest—death has already

stopped mattering to and troubling me—I would like to be able to reflect on all this, on the most important event to have occurred in my life. On Her.

I think of Her and as I do so every phrase, which I speak aloud, since from where I am I don't think I'll be bothering anyone, starts with the same adverb, too, and ends in the same two words, a preposition and a pronoun: for me. She was always: too beautiful for me, too good for me, too rich for me, too wild for me, too young for me, too political for me . . . In short, to consolidate: too much for me. Let's ignore the adjectives, boil it down, stick to the essence, like Beckett. Let's even take away this, the essence, lying at the heart of things, so closely linked to life itself. Let's go further still, take this away too, life itself. I can. I'm dead.

And in this peculiar situation: dead, you must be wondering how it's possible for me to reflect now, from my coffin, here beneath the loose black soil, alongside cypresses that seem to want to touch their canopies to God, like the fingers of that famous hand Michelangelo painted. Aahhh! (horrific surprise), I'm not as dead as you think. Or at least I'm not completely dead . . . or, to put it another way, I'm the project of a dead man, an unfinished dead man.

A demi-dead man.

How is this possible? Oh! It's possible, making use of certain drugs that slow the heart to the point of making its beat so faint for a few hours that it's nearly impossible to detect a pulse and it seems as though the subject in question has died. A small bribe to a certain unscrupulous doctor takes care of the rest. But . . . all this . . . where's the sense in it? What for? Easy, simple, elemental. Why would someone want to be mistaken for a dead man and buried alive in a coffin? To kill himself. To kill himself for love. For the only love possible to me.

To kill himself for Her.

And to have a little time, while killing oneself, to make

certain phone calls, for example, and dictate everything so it
might be set in writing, and to explain along the way how all
these reflections came to be written in the present tense, and
read. To make a certain call to a phone number displayed on
a news clipping which I have in my hand and on which one
may read: writer for hire, I write for you, no signature, at your
service, novels, biographies, any kind of text. I called him a
few minutes ago, or perhaps a few hours, I don't know . . .
(Time, here, on the road to eternity, has, in comparison, little
meaning.) When I called him and explained my situation, at
first he didn't seem to believe me, but no doubt the frigid cold
that was being transmitted from my phone to his and prickling
his ear convinced him. Because the thing is, just like in certain
seashells you can hear the murmur of the sea, in certain phones
you can feel the frigid cold of death (I'm referring of course
to top-notch phones, with high-quality transmission). Then he
said:

"Why are you calling me at this hour?" And I remembered
this phrase as being the title of a song by the band Standstill.

"Breaking a silence like this is unforgivable," I answered,
quoting the song's opening lyrics, and adding:

"In the beyond we don't have schedules."

After my saying this, he excitedly took my commission.
Excited, perhaps, because he was familiar with the song, or
perhaps because—so he told me—he was writing just then, in
the small hours of the night, with a woman sleeping nearby
who said she was his wife, but couldn't have been, though she
looked a lot like her, since his wife had been dead for two years.

"And what did this woman say to explain herself?" I asked,
more from politeness than interest.

"That she's been on the planet Lux all this time and she's
come back, after a nearly endless voyage from the limits of the
universe, just to be with me."

"From the planet Lux," I confirmed.

"Yes," he said.

"Like the vacuum cleaners," I added.

And so, I'm dictating all this from my coffin under the dark, fresh-dug dirt, by the cypresses, and the writer-for-hire is writing, somewhere, beside a sleeping woman who says she's his wife, but who obviously isn't, though she looks eerily like her. Somewhere no doubt very far from the planet Lux.

She, I dictate to the writer-for-hire from my cell phone, was everything to me.

"Was?" asks the writer, and continues, "Then . . . she's dead."

"No," I say.

"Where is she?" he asks.

"Somewhere else, it's far away, abroad," I say.

"Where at exactly?" he insists.

"In the beyond," I say, and then I hear a stifled snicker at the other end of the line and this saddens me. It saddens me to the point of making me depressed, even more than I already am, and also angry, and I tell him I don't find his snickering the least bit funny. In fact I don't find it too fucking funny at all, it's about as fucking funny as a war, as hunger, as your being diagnosed with cancer, as your wife's being diagnosed with cancer, or your son's, as losing hope, as a dead child. Or is it that the business about your wife is funny? I ask, and he's fallen silent and all I hear is nothing. Nothing. As if he were dead. As if he didn't exist.

That sometimes happens.

When you call from a coffin underground sometimes these things happen, sometimes you have coverage problems, or sometimes someone vanishes while you're talking with him, such are the classic dilemmas of conversations from the grave, or perhaps, simply . . .

You've died.

Whatever the case may be, I continue dictating from my cell phone, talking about Her with my mask of Felipe González strapped on tight.

And now, precisely now, that I mention the aged countenance of Felipe González over my own countenance, tight and snug, the elastic string stretched taut, I think about the last words she said to me:

"It's not enough, no, it's not enough—your love. You've ruined my life."

And she left and went far away from me. She went back to her husband, the magnificent medium Walter Solo, and they left for somewhere else. Far away, very far away, beyond (here).

In any case, it was predictable that this story would end badly. It's not a good idea to go to bed with the wife of a medium and above all with the wife of the renowned medium Walter Solo. Even before, long before I walked her home one night, after we chanced to run into each other at a rally, when her husband was out of town attending a conference of famous illusionists, and she invited me to come in and have a drink, knowing that I should decline, but giving in because I was no longer master of my own will, totally subjugated to desire, dazzling desire, long before this, Walter Solo already knew that she would cheat on him with me. Walter Solo knew because Walter Solo knows everything.

Absolutely everything. And I don't know whether to think that he's a cretin, a bastard, or just a man who's lost and hopeless.

Walter Solo knew what Felipe González answered when someone, the sort of lackey who can be someplace without anyone's noticing him, who knows everyone without anyone's knowing him, told him that they had them, that they knew they were going to meet, all of them, the most important ones, but that it was in France and the possibilities of their being arrested there were equal to zero, but that they would all be there, all the top leaders of the E.T.A., that they could blow them up, take out their leadership, that he only had to give the word, that they could do it. That they could kill them all. And

Walter Solo knew Felipe González would say no. And he knew that from that moment on the now ex-president would begin to age by leaps and bounds, torturing himself by tallying each year the number of deaths that could have been avoided.

Walter Solo also knew that I was in France.

Walter Solo also knew that when Felipe González said no, I was saved.

Walter Solo also knew that I killed her father.

Walter Solo also knew that she would find out, that she would discover the documents, the maps of the street where her parents lived, even layouts of the house, and all those letters talking about her father, in my bedroom, that she would discover the gun. The gun I killed her father with.

Walter Solo knew.

Walter Solo knew that She would discover everything in my bedroom and leave me, that she would never tell anyone what I'd done, that she'd go back to him, her husband, and that two nights later in the marriage bed, with that same gun she'd taken from my bedroom, she would put a bullet through her temple. And Walter Solo knew that he would find her there, in the same bed where they had made love so many times, in the same bed where I myself had made love with her, that he would find her there with her head rent open, on white sheets soaked in her blood. The same blood that stained my gun, which Walter himself, streaming with tears, would carefully remove from her hand, opening the fingers clenched in a now involuntary contraction, and point in turn at his own temple.

Walter Solo knew.

Are you listening to me?! I yell at the hack writer over my cell phone, which warns me that little by little its battery is running out. He knew. And now there is certainly not any snickering at the other end of the line, from this point onward there's nothing funny about the story, absolutely nothing. And from here on all that's left is to wait for my battery to run out, and the air, and for me to die. For me to die with my mask of Felipe González strapped tightly to my face, so I'll arrive like this on the other side, abroad, beyond, where She is. And then I'll look fixedly at her from behind my mask, and in my eyes she'll see it's no joke, that none of this is funny, that everything is for her, and I'll say, loudly, in a firm voice: do it. Kill them.

Kill them all.

The Importance of the
Period, New Paragraph

I NEVER LIKED the movies too much. I always preferred reading; in fact the movies I've liked most were always based on novels, and these always seemed superior to their respective film adaptations. Of course, and perhaps for this reason, I haven't bothered very much with movie culture. Having been disappointed time and time again by certain masterpieces, it's gotten to the point where the idea of seeing a movie makes my skin crawl. Why don't we do something else? I always ask, but I never put it so bluntly, not wanting to come off as some kind of weirdo who doesn't like the movies, and whenever people ask me which ones I like, I always cite that masterpiece by Stanley Kubrick, which, as it happens, is perhaps the only movie that surpasses the book on which it's based.

2001: A Space Odyssey.

"Fuck me," they say, and they immediately regret having spoken, because they think that I think that they're unable to think, or at least that thinking makes their skin crawl. Then they think but, instructed this time by their first mistake, don't say:

"But it's impossible to understand."

And that's exactly why I bring it up, because I know I won't be asked any more questions, because I know that now the conversation about film is over. End of conversation, change of direction. Period, new paragraph.

It's like at those couples' dinners where the visiting couple, whom you've come to regret inviting, never leave, because they're talking on and on about themselves, about their house, about their upcoming vacation, about the one after that, about all of them, about the children they're going to have, about what kind of school they'll go to, about their life in forty years, and then, interrupting them all of a sudden, I say: "Now then, why don't we go to the bedroom and swap partners!" End of conversation, change of direction. Period, new paragraph.

Once they said yes. End of conversation, change of direction. Period, new paragraph, too.

And now I'm going to tell you about the time they said yes, I could write at this point, since I'm jotting down all of what's happening to me in order to write a story that will be part of my future book of short stories, which is, in turn, my chaotic and disorganized autobiography. I'm sure this is what the reader would like most. That I write this phrase that fits perfectly with what's been related so far. But I won't do it. I won't do it because maybe I could save it for the final part of this story, to hold the reader's interest, or maybe for another story altogether, which obviously I'll place at the end of the book which "The Importance of the Period, New Paragraph" is a part of, and which I will hypothetically call "The Time They Said Yes."

I never really liked *2001: A Space Odyssey*, and the reason I didn't like it, to be frank, was that I never understood it at all. The fact is, my favorite movie, which I never admit to, since it doesn't say much in my favor, stars Wesley Snipes. In my defense, I should also mention that it's the only Wesley Snipes movie I like, and to generalize a little more, even if it sounds obscene to the lovers of the absurdly named seventh art, I can truly say that it's the only movie I like. It's called *One Night Stand*, and Wesley Snipes's work in this particular film won him the prize for best actor at the Venice Film Festival. Which I also submit here in my defense, or else to the detriment of the Venice Film Festival, I'm not altogether sure which.

The thing is, I've mentioned my favorite movie *One Night*

Stand because, like its protagonist, strangely enough, I'm preparing to go to another city to see my friend, we might as well call him that, who's dying, and who also happens to be gay, like the character played by Robert Downey Jr. in the movie. And just like in the movie, I expect to find a woman there with a certain likeness to Nastassja Kinski, a friend of my friend, to miss my return flight, and to spend the night with her, tormented by the doubts resulting from my infidelity.

I don't really know how *One Night Stand* ends. I don't know how it ends because before seeing it for the first time I leafed through the newspaper to read some review and came across this: A dense magma of spontaneity which at first surprises you, then hooks you in, and in the end (more's the pity) lets you down. Easy, I thought to myself at the time, I won't see the end, which I didn't, and now as I think back on all this, I'm preparing to board a plane that will take me to the bedside of my, let's call him my dying gay friend Max, where I'll find myself with her, a woman resembling, for sure, Nastassja Kinski, and spend the night with her, tormented by my infidelity, and I'll write the ending this time, my own imaginary and no doubt grandiose ending, of *One Night Stand*.

Sometimes there are roads that take you somewhere you'd never expected; sometimes there are couples' dinners that end in a way you'd never expected; sometimes there are planes that take you to a night you'd never expected.

To this night, here in this hospital room in this unfamiliar city, at the side of my friend Max who's dying, and at the sides of his closest friends, among whom there isn't a single woman who even slightly resembles Nastassja Kinski, in fact there isn't a single woman here at all. This entire, absurdly dramatic scene, all of these supposedly gay friends of Max's, talking about everything that's happened to them, all those wonderful things, all they've been through together. Everyone here crying for Max, even I find myself crying, although in my case, of course, it's not for Max, but Nastassja Kinski.

Then there's Max, he's crying too, crying with his last strength, his last tears, with all that's left of himself, because by now he has the absolute certainty—as do all of us around him—that whatever he does, he does for the last time. Max cries and says he's afraid, afraid of dying, and although I think it's somewhat late for that now, that he should have thought of that earlier, already have cleared that up, I don't say so. Instead, I tell him not to think about death, suggesting he think instead about all his friends gathered here who love him, who love him very much. Then I realize I'm the only one talking, and that everyone else is looking devastated and is whimpering, crying, or bellowing like an animal, and I feel out of place, and noticing this, Max calls me over. I move closer and he takes my hand, I don't know why. Doubtless, of all of us here, I know him less than anyone. As he holds my hand, he thanks me for my calmness, saying he understands, thanking me for not showing my pain so he might be calmer. As he says this, his voice almost lifeless, the others' weeping grows unbearable. I agree with him, parroting back that I'm trying to endure calmly, for his sake, the pain of his departure, but my only thought is of Nastassja Kinski. Then, with eyes full of pure terror, he says he has one last wish, and grips my hand tighter. I tell him he's in no condition to sleep with me, at which he smiles weakly, and the others, seeing his forced smile in all his pain and horror, bellow even louder. And Max brings his face as close to me as he can and says he wants to be buried near the sea, next to a pine tree, a giant pine like the one in mom's garden, and within his coffin to be wrapped in white sheets, washed with Marseilles soap, like mom's sheets, and to be buried in an Ibizan groom's suit, and for a few pots of lavender to be planted by his tomb. And then a doctor appears in the room and rushes over to us as a high-pitched beeping tone starts sounding on and off, and the others bellow even louder with their faces covered in spittle and snot, and there's Max squeezing my hand so tight it almost hurts, while the doctor cuts open his shirt, exposing his emaciated chest, and injects him with something, and then Max writhes and blanches pure white and the tendons in his neck become taut and all of a sudden he's still. Very still, his eyes wide open, looking at me. And Max is no longer here with us. He's gone, left for somewhere else, somewhere far away, he's gone abroad, he's in the beyond.

And as if someone had thrown a switch, everyone falls silent, his friends stop bellowing and exit the room in total silence, and although I want to more than anything, I'm unable to leave, because Max's hand, still warm though I imagine it to be already gloomily frozen, won't let go of me.

You've got to be shitting me.

You've got to be shitting me, and to think I'd imagined myself comforting Nastassja Kinski.

"You've got to be shitting me," says the doctor beside me in the hallway, after managing, with the aid of another doctor and a nurse, to pry me free of Max's hand. "You've got to be shitting me," he continues saying, "they can't die one after the other, no, they both have to do it at the same time." And I look at the half-open door from which the doctor who says this has just emerged, thinking now you've really got to be shitting me, as well as that now would be a good time to open my notebook and talk about what happened after that couples' dinner, after that time when, completely fed up with my guests' yakking I blurted out that so what if we go to the bedroom and swap partners! business. And they answered yes. The story about "The Time They Said Yes." So I'm getting ready to talk about this when, out of curiosity, I go into the room next door, where the other doctor came from and where the other man who died at the same time as Max must be, and inside . . .

Inside I see a dead man wearing a mask of Felipe González.

Inside I see a dead man wearing a mask of Felipe González,

who gets out of his bed, staggering as if drugged, and tiptoes to a chair, where there's a coat from which he takes a cell phone that he puts in the pocket of his pajama bottoms, and who returns, again on tiptoe, to his bed, to play dead once more, or at any rate, to continue being dead, after this brief and unexpected resurgence of life.

You've got to be shitting me.

I no longer feel in the mood, or in the optimal state to tell the story about "The Time They Said Yes," so I go back to . . . oh let's call him my dead gay friend Max, to put everything in order.

"Everyone's gone, Max," I say, "all your friends, and here I am, who at bottom really know almost nothing about you.

"So, Max," I also say, "there's nothing left for me to do but to put everything in order. I owe it to you. I'll do it, for your sake."

I say this, and stand there for a moment thinking about the other dead man. About the dead man with the mask of Felipe González, who isn't so dead. I think of the fleeting instant when his eyes looked, from behind the mask, at mine. And here, in my notebook, I find it impossible to describe those eyes. All I can do, anyway, is note what they made me feel, what they suggested to me. They suggested cold. An icy, brutal cold, like walking naked through snow.

Like walking naked through snow, after a cold shower.

Like walking naked through snow, after a cold shower, while eating sugar-free lemon ice cream.

Like walking naked through snow, after a cold shower, while eating sugar-free lemon ice cream and having the absolute certainty that God does not exist.

Like being dead. Dead and buried. And without lemon ice cream.

Speaking of which, that business about burying Max by the sea, under a giant pine tree, like in mom's garden, all that about the white sheets perfumed with Marseilles soap, and the Ibizan groom's suit and the pots of lavender: nothing came of all that. Not one thing. I simply burn him. Now, I'm in the waiting room of this enormous and impersonal crematorium, waiting for Max to incinerate, to burn until he turns to ash, without his white suit, his pine tree, his fragrant sheets, or his lavender.

At least this way he won't feel the icy cold of death.

And now, as I wait for my dead gay friend Max, as we're calling him, to be reduced to ash, I think, reclining on this soft leather sofa, in this enormous room, on this floor of stony marble tiles, that now is a good time to tell the story about "The Time They Said Yes." I think it's about time I told it, and it will be a good way to pass the time while I wait for Max's emaciated body to burn to a crisp and disintegrate, be reduced to nothing, or almost nothing. So I'll tell the story about "The Time They Said Yes." The story of that dinner to which we invited Max and his girlfriend at the time, none other, since back then Max was still living a lie, the great lie that was his life until he decided to finally give it a period, new paragraph. To come out of the closet (that's what people say, isn't it?).

But before I continue, I'd like to emphasize the importance of the period, new paragraph. The vital importance of the period, new paragraph, with which one brings to a close a section of text or, as Max did, one of life, in order to start another paragraph that's distinct, different, that moves forward again, but in another direction. I'd like to emphasize the importance of the period, new paragraph that involved my saying:

"And now why don't we go to the bedroom and swap partners!" End of conversation, change of direction. Period, new paragraph.

With this, I had wanted to alter the course of the night, to modify the direction things were moving in. To slightly change the course of my life. Not change it completely. Not destroy it.

I'd like to emphasize, here and now, the enormous importance of the period, new paragraph.

The importance, also, of the fact that you, Max—now I shift toward writing for you, narrating these events for you alone—were the first one to say before everyone's stupefaction and silence:

"Yes, let's do it."

And you said yes because you wanted to be with me, because you'd spent the whole night wanting to be with me, turning a deaf ear to all the things that girl was saying, that girl who chattered on and on. You took the first step, saying yes, while we'd all been staring at each other in silence. Then your girlfriend, that poor young girl . . . she was hardly twenty, wasn't she Max? spoke up in a weak voice: yes. And as she gave her answer she was looking at you, Max, seeking your approval, seeking for your satisfied gaze to rest on her, like the hand that pets a dog. Because that girl was in love with you, Max. She was crazy about you . . . how could you have been so cruel? And then my wife, my wife whom I loved, whom I'd never cheated on with anyone, and whom I'd never thought capable of such a thing, also said it: yes. She said yes, and destroyed my life. She said yes, and I yelled out, no! I yelled out no and everything stopped being like it was. End of conversation, change of direction. Period, new paragraph.

And now, dear Max, I, for my part, set down here, at last, the final period, while you, without a pine tree nearby or a white Ibizan groom's suit, without sheets that smell like Marseilles soap or pots of lavender, burn, are reduced to ash, burn and are reduced to the smallest nothing of your ashes, as though you were in hell.

Amnesic Recollections
of Christ and the Hitchhiking Girl

CHRIST WAS A woman, or at least the new vision of Christ was, the remix of Christ, accompanied by guitar riffs. And here, in this story I'm writing, I intend to approach this figure. That of her. And I intend to look back across time, through the distortions typical of a memory that has forgotten nearly everything. So I might end up altering a few dates, a few facts, even take myself for someone else, perhaps. It's even possible I'll put down sentences I think I've invented, but which are merely plagiaries of sentences already written by others. Sentences like this one:

Ever since the newspapers started saying that the world is going to end, songs have seemed shorter and the days longer.

Sentences like this one, by Ray Loriga, a sentence that, in turn, Loriga wrote believing it was his, thinking he was creating it, but which in fact he'd just freshly forgotten.

Ray Loriga strikes me as a good writer. He's been much criticized. Such things have been said about him as: it would be for the best if he dropped literature and dedicated himself to writing lyrics for punk bands. But now that the days are longer and songs, whatever the genre, all seem shorter, I'm not sure how to take this. There are some very good punk songs. Songs like the ones she, Christ, used to write—and to sing.

Those same songs I would listen to as I was speeding along in my car. The same punk songs of hers, of Christ's, that I was listening to in my car one day, hurtling down the highway, when I rolled down the window and threw out of it the best gift—I now have to admit—that anyone had ever given me:

the novel *Heroes*, by Ray Loriga, which had been a present from her, Christ, and was underlined and annotated in tiny, cramped handwriting, which compared its protagonist to me, and the blond girl found in its pages to herself.

I don't listen to those songs anymore. I don't even listen to all the ones that Ray Loriga listened to, locked in a room writing *Heroes*. I no longer listen to Dylan, or Bowie, or Jagger. I listen to Tool now, songs like "Eulogy," or "H," or "Sober," which are what this story intends to be like, something advancing toward an unknown destination, through other memories wholly distinct from those of the beginning, and which sharply veers down detours toward other places where I never thought it could go.

So I move ahead, with my writing, toward an unknown destination, taking sharp turns that make my speeding car shudder recklessly, listening to "H" on the CD player, heading down unexpected detours and secondary roads that take me somewhere I never could have expected.

Somewhere like this house. This dark house that gives off a shut-in smell as if it had never been lived in, or perhaps more as if its inhabitants had been locked inside for years and years until they died of starvation and their bodies were now no more than these bones I'm walking across, which crunch beneath my feet. The house of the hitchhiking girl.

"Just to look at you, anyone would think those bones you're stepping on were human," the hitchhiking girl says, and the way her long body moves, it's as if she were dancing to "Across the Universe," insofar as that song can be danced to.

Then, she tells me that these bones belonged to her cats, which had died a long time ago and which she had not wanted to bury, since to bury them would have been like removing them permanently from her life, certifying their inscrutable death as something that was done with and forgotten. So she decided to keep their bones, bathing their feline corpses in a special kind of acid, so she could then scatter their tiny femurs and shins over the living room floor. This way, whenever she stepped on them, the little sounds they made would comfort her, in the same way that she was once comforted by the purrs and meows of her now quite inseparable pets. And this, she says, is what she would like me to do with her own bones, if she dies before I do. She says this with the familiarity you would use to talk to someone you've shared your life with. Because the hitchhiking girl says that spending our lives together is just what we'll be doing. She also says that she knows me, knows me very well.

I don't remember anything, and it's possible that this lapse in memory is only a defense mechanism, or maybe an act of self-deception to help me deny something I have some sense of, but still can't manage to remember.

I've already given fair warning that I'll be looking back through the distortions of a memory that has forgotten nearly everything. A memory that clings to a few certainties, to be used for the construction of a framework, a rubric, a few notes toward a novel that would at least be called *My Life*. A few certainties, not many. For instance, that Christ was a woman and played in a punk band; Christ was a woman, a punk musician, and made a gift to me of Ray Loriga's novel *Heroes*, which she had underlined and annotated herself.

And Christ had big green eyes that remind me very much of the green eyes of the hitchhiking girl who says she knows me, loves me, and is going to spend the rest of her life with me, until she dies, until I douse her with acid and scatter her white bones over the living room floor and slow-dance over them listening to an old record by, for example, John Coltrane, so that I'll remember her until my very last, and no doubt consoling, breath.

All this from the hitchhiking girl I picked up on some byroad.

"I'm too connected to you to slip away, to fade away,"
she had said, as she swung her long body into my car, which
was pulled over on the shoulder of the road with the motor
running. She said this over the guitar chords that came just
before Maynard James Keenan would sing the exact same
words she'd just spoken, and he went on: "Days away, I still feel
you / Touching me, changing me, / And considerately killing
me." And it was then I understood that one way or another
the hitchhiking girl was somehow connected to me, and at the
same time to her as well, to Christ, and she talked to me of very
strange things as I drove along the winding roads through the
dusk fog. Things which at first made no sense, only to take on
great significance, to mean everything, when they were echoed
by Tool's lead singer over my car speakers, and I came to link
them up with the unconnected, tortured memories of my past
life with Christ.

For a second I even began to think that the hitchhiking girl
was she, Christ.

For a second I thought this, and that's why I kept quiet as
she was saying what Maynard James Keenan would then sing
after a few seconds' delay, and I stayed quiet as I pulled up to
her house, veiled in fog somewhere at the end of a lost byroad
in the middle of nowhere. Because of this sneaking suspicion,
I believed everything she told me in the living room of this
house as the bones of her defunct cats crunched beneath my
feet, as she spoke at length about our future life together, as
her body moved as if dancing to "Across the Universe." For a
second I began to think she was Christ, while her long body
was swaying like a serpent's over mine later that night, and her
panting breaths came like hisses in the dirty sheets, with the
damp stains on the walls coalescing into shapes that seemed
like scenes from the Bible. For a second—fleetingly, but with
the relative fleetingness seconds have when mired in still night
fog—I thought she was Christ. So I thought, until I came out

and asked her if it was true and she froze, stopped swaying and hissing, and began to speak very slowly, saying something I didn't understand but which seemed like a prayer, and I took an apple that, inexplicably, she was offering me and bit into it, and when I did, at that exact instant, the hitchhiking girl coughed and from her mouth a little blood spurted out. I asked if she was all right. Covering her nakedness with the sheets, she said she was fine, it was just that now she felt confused, confused and foolish, because for a moment she had thought I'd forgotten about her, about Christ, and that we would both forget about her once and for all, and live in peace together like in the beginning, forever, but she realizes that it was all just false hope.

So now we're in my car, hurtling through the night fog, listening to the music of Tool. It was her idea to go for a drive, because this way, she says, she can have the illusion that it's not we who are moving, but the things whirring past us through the middle of the night. This way, she says, maybe everything will speed away from us and get left behind, everything, even my memories. And when she says this, I tell her that memories are never left behind, no matter how fast you drive down secondary roads, I tell her that memories always survive, like parasites on the skin of a corpse, until they find something living to latch on to and revive. It's then she says that sometimes, if you drive too fast through the fog at night, you could run over someone walking down the middle of the road, someone who seems to be alive, but who's really nothing but a dead man walking in the middle of the night, lost in the despair of feeling that for him there's no future, and therefore no life, which makes him already dead.

"What are you trying to say?" I ask, taken aback by her cryptic talk.

And just then she tells me to stop, saying there's someone in front of us, and I don't see anyone, but she's screaming:

"Stop! Stop! There's somebody out there!"

But between the fog and dark I can't see anything, and shout back, Who? Who? and step on the brakes as hard as I can, in the same instant that she unbuckles her seatbelt and says:

"Me," and she's launched against the windshield, which shatters, and goes straight through it, flying outside, into the final darkness.

I get out of the car, my face covered in blood from having hit something, and go over to kneel down by her motionless body, sprawled in the light of my car's headlights. I look into her open eyes, while from the car speakers the voice of Maynard James Keenan recites: "And the snake is drowned and / As I look in his eyes, / My fear begins to fade / Recalling all of those times. / I could have cried then. / I should have cried then. / And as the walls come down, / And as I look in your eyes, / My fear begins to fade / Recalling all of those times / I have died / And will die. / It's all right. / I don't mind."

The rest, what happens next, is, to put it one way, a long epitaph. A long epitaph, which I won't describe here in detail, but which includes a man, who is me, taking a long trek down the middle of a deserted highway, in the middle of the night and fog, carrying the hitchhiking girl's inert body. It also includes the detailed description of some large bottles of acid which the man (who is me) finally comes across after an exhaustive search through the basement of the hitchhiking girl's house, and which he empties into the bathtub. Likewise, and this should explain why I'm not giving a running commentary of this long epitaph, besides its being somewhat self-indulgent, I will leave out a description of the bloody dismemberment, which it includes as well, that I carried out on the hitchhiking girl so she could be entirely covered by the acid in her own bathtub.

There are things it's better to leave out.

Like certain gory details (someone should have told Tarantino this when he started making sub-par movies).

Things I'd rather leave out but which, instead (like the following), I won't leave out, because I have to describe them so that the facts will lead me, in this writing that moves forward, taking sharp, unforeseen turns, to some conclusions about these pages which act as a framework, built up out of the hazy certainties upon which I base my existence. In short, there are facts I won't leave out, because of their importance in my life, ones I have to reflect on, and draw my conclusions from. Facts which of themselves are sharp turns in this unforeseen narration, facts like the visit from the vacuum salesman.

The vacuum salesman is very tall, extremely tall and very thin, seeming as though at any moment he could snap in two. He's so tall and bizarre-looking that I comment on how he doesn't seem like he's from around here.

"You don't look like you're from this area," I say, letting him inside with his sample vacuum cleaner.

"That's because I'm not, although I've lived here for many years now, I was born on the planet Lux," he says. "And speaking of which," he goes on, "that's where we manufacture these magnificent Electrolux vacuum cleaners."

I show him into the living room with his interplanetarily imported vacuum cleaner and tell him that I maybe ought to buy a vacuum cleaner from him, and I inform him that he doesn't need to bother going on about the technical benefits of the model in question, that although I think he's crazy or that he's trying to screw around with some convoluted sales strategy, it makes no difference to me, because I really do need a vacuum cleaner, mainly to vacuum up all the dust accumulating amidst the bones on the floor. I also tell him not to make that face, they're not human bones, of course, they're cat bones.

"They're a memento," I say.

"Yeah," he says, "it's normal," he adds, and I stand there staring at him, trying to figure out what he meant by that.

"But, since I'm here," he says, talking slowly, as if measuring his words, "and since you're the kind of person who has bones scattered all over the living room floor, that is, let's put it this way: you're not an ordinary guy, perhaps you might be interested in another line of services that I can offer."

"Services like what?" I ask.

"Services like reviving a dead person," he says, and I look at him again, fixedly, and realize my current situation: I am in a solitary house lost in the middle of nowhere with a lunatic who says he can revive the dead, and with the quartered cadaver, submerged in acid, of a woman in the bathroom.

"By the way, where's the bathroom?" asks the vacuum salesman. "Thing is, I've got prostate trouble," he adds.

So here we are, and since I always liked writing, I'll show off my status as a talented budding writer and tell a story that, given its literary quality, will come off as plausible, however strange it at first may seem. So I tell the vacuum salesman I'm a promising young movie director, experimenting with a transgressive new method of filming.

"So what's the movie about?" he asks.

"It's about a guy with amnesia, who unintentionally runs over a woman he knows, and according to her last will he puts her in a bathtub full of acid, so only her bones are left, which he then has to scatter over the living room floor of her house. And it's all filmed by small cameras hidden in the nooks and crannies of the house that are controlled by off-site operators," I tell him.

"Right," he says.

Then I ask him if he remembers that movie by Tarantino, the one called *Reservoir Dogs*. The only good movie by that director, I clarify, where the lurid details are in a certain measure omitted. The lurid details like when Michael Madsen, who plays Mr. Blonde, is dancing to the song "Stuck In The Middle With You" holding a knife in his hand and moving toward a police officer that he's got gagged and tied to a chair, and just as he's about to cut the guy's ear off, the camera swivels and focuses elegantly on the wall, while the music keeps playing and blends with the other man's screams.

"Well then," I tell him, "when you go into the bathroom to pee, you must not, like the camera that will film that scene, look at the bathtub where there's a woman's body, which has been quartered and immersed in acid."

"Right," he says, and slowly, as if trying to maintain an impossible balance with each step of his extremely long and skinny legs, below which the bones on the floor are crunching, he heads toward where I've indicated that the bathroom is.

When he returns a few minutes later, he sits down beside me on the sofa and looks into my eyes for a long time, and then he tells me that, of course, he never believed all that about the movie director and the experimental film, but deep down he believes that I'm not a bad person and that horrible things, like running over a woman, dismembering her, and dousing her with acid sometimes happen without anyone's wanting them to. He also tells me that deep down I want him to revive the woman and take her to the planet Lux—where the revived dead go, he explains—and from where, after a certain amount of time spent working off the debt of having been brought back from the dead in one Electrolux factory or other, she could come back, after an extraordinarily long interstellar journey, to Earth. But—and as he says this he looks heavily at me, as though he were saying something that he didn't want to say, as though he were a doctor telling you that you have cancer, Alzheimer's, or any other horrible thing—given the state of decomposition and dismemberment the cadaver is in, it will be impossible for him to employ any of his advanced techniques for bringing her back to life.

I, truly moved and on the verge of tears for the kindness and understanding of the extremely tall vacuum salesman, give him a hug and say, by now in tears, that in any case I still need the vacuum cleaner. He, also moved, no doubt by my tears, says

very well, he'll give me a good price, an excellent price, and
show me how to use it. He gestures toward the cat bones on the
floor and tells me that I'll see how white they're going to be. He
switches on the vacuum cleaner, equipping it with its special
filter for cleaning cat bones and it really does leave them white,
extremely white. As white as if they were those human bones
you sometimes see in horror movies.

"These aren't cat bones," the vacuum salesman suddenly
says, "they're fractured human bones."

"What?" I say.

"As a matter of fact, the hairs stuck to some of these bones
aren't exactly feline," he says, showing me a long blond hair that
he disentangles from the filter of the vacuum.

"A hair exactly like Christ's long blond hair," I think and,
unintentionally, say out loud.

"What?" says the vacuum salesman.

"What! What! What!" I scream, and all of a sudden, like
an explosion, like a shock, like a brutal electrical discharge, I
remember everything. Everything, the whole kit and caboodle
comes flooding back to my mind. I remember Christ in those
days following 15 May 2011, in her house, in this same house,
after getting back from Madrid. After coming back with her,
in her van, my wife and I, after the demonstrations and the
altercations of that 15 May 2011. After feeling lost, on the
verge of eviction, mortgaged to the hilt, screaming, against
something, but without knowing exactly what.

Something we weren't at all too certain of. And for a
moment we were quite surprised to be hearing our own screams
of hatred. Of hatred against something, something horrible,
against which everyone was screaming.

Everyone was screaming and there was a huge amount of
noise. Madrid was noise. Noise and pent-up rage, a rage against
everything and against nothing. Then she, Christ, appeared.
She started to speak in a powerful voice. So powerful it seemed

unnatural in this skinny girl with long blond hair. She started to talk about the system, cry out against the system, and point the finger in all directions, finding culprits for us to direct our rage at amidst all that noise.

There was an unbelievable amount of noise, but her voice imposed itself over everything. Over everyone. And I was so scared and only wanted to find someone in this confused world to identify with, someone who would tell me what I had to do, someone who would show me the way, someone who would show me what to fight against, and she showed me the system and the offices across the street, and the riot police gathering in front of the crowd in positions of—attack? Defense? So I shouted out to her, to Christ, asking if she would die for us.

"Will you die for us?" we shouted.

"Will you die for me?" I shouted, and someone held out a metal rod to her, to Christ, and she threw herself into the riot squad and then everything descended into chaos and there were screams and smoke and blood. And then we found ourselves, hours later, in someone's house, someone who played guitar in her, Christ's, punk band, where we dressed and disinfected each other's wounds. Afterward we drank, we drank a lot, the four of us there in the guitarist's house, he, Christ, my wife, and I. And when we were done drinking, Christ sang lyrics of hatred and fire, while the other played guitar, and there was fire, inside me—fire. Then we left the guitarist's house and got into Christ's rundown van, and she drove us out of the city and down highway after highway, each one more secondary than the last, more twisting and lost, while we talked about putting an end to the system, while she said that in order to build you first must destroy. Destroy everything.

And we arrived at her house, the three of us. Christ, my wife, and I. My wife, the hitchhiking girl.

And we talked about revolution and told her, Christ, that we would follow her. And we spent the days there burning, wanting something to happen, preparing ourselves for we didn't really know what. We were there for days, until the evening came when she gave me, in secret and without my wife's seeing it, the novel *Heroes*, by Ray Loriga, which she had underlined and annotated herself, comparing herself to that blond girl in the novel and myself to its protagonist. And then, later that night, after a lot of drinking, which had left us all very intoxicated, and after screaming slogans against everything, throwing blame on all but ourselves, my wife the hitchhiking girl, the worse for wear, fell asleep in front of the fireplace, and I gazed steadily, then, at Christ and asked her if she would die for me.

"Would you die for me?" I said, and she said: yes. And kissed me. I felt a fire in my lips and pressed my body to hers, until she started screaming at the top of her lungs, until the blood from her split head sprayed in my face, and I turned around and there was another fire burning, in the eyes of my wife, who lifted the heavy bronze lamp high above her head and brought it down, once more, on Christ's skull, which made a cracking sound, and her blood spilled out over all of us.

The Irish Sea
(Exactly 27%)

THIS IS WHERE the seed is, in the past, at the beginning of everything, at the beginning of this book, which moves ahead like a life written in an autobiography. An autobiography of someone else.

1.

Interesting things only happen in dark corners. He thinks about this sentence that he heard once as he moves away from the chatter and smoke toward the blackness of that corner of the pub. There's a small door there that he can just make out in the darkness. He opens it and goes inside without looking, closing the door behind him. Inside, the space is so small that his own body barely fits. The walls are made of wood, he can tell by their rough texture, the lines between the slats, and the smell of them under the alcohol on his own breath. He tries the door again, but it doesn't open. He's locked inside, and then, the terror sets in. Javier understands that the small wood-paneled room to the measure of his own body is none other than his coffin. At the consciousness of his death, he's dogged by a despair that envelops him until at last Javier opens his eyes.

The room is dark. This is what death is like, he thinks: to be lying in a bed in total silence, total absence of light. Then he hears a faint voice on the other side of the door. It's his wife saying something. She's talking to the kids. Then he hears their childish voices, too. He sits up in bed, reaches for the curtain, and pulls it open a little, letting in the light. The light of the world of the living. He considers getting up, but doesn't. The world of the dead has caught hold of his thoughts, and he lies there for a while, this side of the bedroom door, the side of the dead, or of those awakening, as he is, from the world of the dead. Then, as he's waking up, so does the awareness that he's going to die. He thinks of how it seems like yesterday that he was a boy putting himself to sleep by trying not to think, and in order not to think of anything, he would have to fill his mind with a single thought: rocky coasts battered by the wind, and a dark sea. Like yesterday, and now he's thirty-three years old: he's lived nearly half his life. Maybe he could fall asleep right now and wake up thirty-three years older, sixty-six, and then he'd think about death, about how he'd no longer be able to fall asleep and expect to wake up again, on this side at least, that of the living. He mulls all this over and once again feels the despair he felt in his dream. To get rid of it and think of something else, he picks up the book lying on the bedside table. He opens to the part that's been bookmarked. He doesn't remember which paragraph he'd left his reading at, so he chooses one at random. He chooses the last complete paragraph on page one hundred and forty-six of *Dublinesque* and reads:

He has the impression that absolutely everything is new to him, even the steps he takes, the ground he walks on, the air he breathes. If everyone knew how to see the world like this, he thinks, if everyone understood that maybe everything around us can be new, we wouldn't need to waste time thinking about death.

Reading this, Javier feels ashamed of himself. It's as if life, the world of the living, were laughing at him. Javier doesn't believe in destiny, or coincidences for that matter, but he makes up his mind to leave that same day, instead of the next, as he'd planned. He needs everything to be new now, or at least that's what he needs to be thinking of.

When he says goodbye, he touches his wife. He kisses her,

hugs her, but this doesn't affect him at all, instead what does affect him is the touch of her hand on his face, making him feel a terrible remorse. An anxiety at the approaching betrayal, at the touch, the smell, the taste of another skin. A new skin. To keep her from seeing this in his eyes, he turns to his children and hugs them.

The highway carries him in the direction of Barcelona. He listens to the song "Por Enésima Vez" (For the Umpteenth Time) twenty times on the CD player over the course of the drive. He thinks that he, too, for the umpteenth time today has taken stock of his situation.

He arrives at Sitges before nightfall. She's not there yet. She'll come tomorrow, as they'd agreed. He goes up to his room in the hotel he's picked out: the Port Sitges Resort. The hotel is by the port of Aiguadolç, and the rooms that look out over the water from the rocky coast seem almost literally on the sea. This sea, which, from the large bay window of his room, reminds him of the sea from his childhood thoughts.

In bed now, after the solitude of a few beers at the hotel bar, the last thing Javier reads before going to sleep is the following paragraph:

He changed his language to impoverish his expression. And in the end his texts appeared more and more purged. The lucid delirium of poverty. Going through life forever hindered, precarious, inert, deformed, unsettled, numb, terrified, unwelcomed, naked, sickly, shaky, defenseless, exiled, inconsolable, playful. Beckett, skinny and smoking in his room in Tiers-Temps, a nursing home in Paris. His pockets full of cake for the pigeons. Retired, like any other elderly person with no family, to an old people's home. Thinking of the Irish Sea. Waiting for the final darkness. "Much better, in the end, if sorrow disappears and silence returns. In the end, it's how you've always been. Alone."

Javier reads on for another sentence, in the end, but it doesn't register, and he replaces it in his fading consciousness with another:

Alone. So far from the Irish Sea.

He closes his eyes, the inert book, without the life the reader endows it with, falls on his chest, and at the exact instant when the world of dreams wraps him up, trying to pull him down, for a few hours, into the infinite solitude of the dreamer, Javier understands that the sea he once thought of as a child just before falling asleep was the same dark sea—menacing, but at the same time intoxicating—that Samuel Beckett had thought of, as he smoked in his room at the Tiers-Temps nursery home.

His cell phone rings. It's her, his lover. He goes down to the front desk, she's not there. He walks outside and sees her. Elena is standing there looking at him, her red suitcase on the ground beside her. The taxi that brought her fades away over the street's horizon, heading, most likely, for Barcelona. She's wearing a long skirt and a leather jacket. He goes over to her. Her face, at only an inch's distance from his own, looks ravaged. This last month has been hard on her—on him, too. He thinks to himself that she must be divvying up her deterioration between her body's inside and outside. He, on the other hand, keeps it all locked up deep in the pit of his stomach. He takes her face in his hands and kisses her, feeling her lips and her tongue. Breathing in her scent, as if it were the last breath of air in his life.

Now Elena and Javier are walking along the cliff road that goes from the hotel to downtown Sitges. The wind is cold and she's shivering; Javier hugs her in a vain attempt at imparting some warmth to her. Frozen, they look at the sea as they walk. The sky is growing dark, and the waves roaring against the rocks. She moves a few steps ahead of him, staring down raptly at the waves. He watches her. The sea in the background is definitely no longer the Mediterranean; no, this is the Irish Sea. This sea that feels like his own. And they aren't in Sitges anymore, they're in Smerwick Bay. Instead of the Port Sitges Resort, they're staying at the Smerwick Harbour Hotel, near Dingle. And there, in Ireland, is where he wants to stay, with her, even though he knows it's all impossible, and that in a few days he must go back to his wife and children. He considers everything and wants to scream, he wants to scream at the sea, at the wind, he wants Elena to hear the passion in his voice, his pain, his human right, the exaltation of his existence, he wants to start screaming an I, intoning an I as a kind of banner, an exclamation of his own being as something unique and apart. He thinks all this, but keeps silent. No scream whatsoever escapes his lips; he bows his head, dejected, having remembered Ortega y Gasset's old sentence: I am I and my circumstances.

Later on, after getting back, in the hotel room. Elena, perhaps a little drunk from all the red wine they'd enjoyed, standing up, facing him, who's sitting on the bed, says:

"I've left my husband."

He stares at her. She doesn't want to hold his gaze and turns to the bay window.

"Did you leave him because of me?" Javier then asks.

"Think whatever you want," she answers, not taking her eyes off the horizon.

Javier looks at the sea as well. He doesn't go over to her. He doesn't want to know if there are tears in her eyes. He couldn't stand to look at them, so he doesn't. Instead, he looks at the infinite Irish Sea.

2.

Javier is once again walking with Elena along the cliff road. They've left the Smerwick Harbour Hotel early and are heading toward Dingle for dinner, taking a peaceful walk, looking at the calm, quiet, threatening beauty of those waters that draw in

Javier as if they were sirens, making him feel like Ulysses—not the Ulysses of Homer, however, but that other one from the story by Kafka with that beautiful sentence:

Now the sirens have a still more terrible weapon than their song, namely their silence.

And that's what Javier feels like, faced with its silence. The calm, voracious silence that calls to him from the most unfathomable depths of this sea, his sea. He would throw himself into it without a moment's hesitation in order to rock tenderly in a descent, which he pictures as an ovarian descent, to the root, to the mother, to the beginning, the primeval. But he doesn't do it, he doesn't throw himself into the sea, because of her, who, like the mast, draws her Ulysses toward herself with those iron chains of dense love.

They have a long time left before dinner, so Javier decides to wander a little way from the road and heads some distance down another of the cliff-side paths. There they come to a small courtyard, in the middle of which stands a stone monolith. Elena lets go of Javier's hand and walks over to inspect this strange monument. There are twelve heads carved in the stone. Elena turns around to Javier, smiling at him questioningly.

"Actually, it wasn't twelve, more like six hundred," says Javier.

"Well, well . . . So what happened here?" she asks.

Javier relates the story to her. She listens closely. He looks at her green eyes, and as he starts to speak, thinks to himself that there isn't a thing he wouldn't do for this woman.

"It all started on the tenth of September, 1580, when six hundred soldiers, some Italian, but for the most part Spanish, under the command of Sebastiano di San Giuseppe, disembarked at Smerwick Bay, having been financed and dispatched there by Pope Gregory XIII to aid in the Irish Catholics' rebellion against the English Protestants. But after several months garrisoned in Smerwick Fort, waiting for reinforcements that never came, they were surprised by more than four thousand

British soldiers who had them totally surrounded, by land and by sea. Even though the Spanish soldiers could have held out for much longer, the siege was a brief one, because Sebastiano di San Giuseppe surrendered to the English after only three days, counting on their benevolence. And having to eliminate several of his own who were against the surrender, going so far as crucifying two Spanish priests. So, on the tenth of October the troops of Lord Grey Wilton entered the fort. And he gave the order to massacre all the defeated Spanish, Italians, and Irish who had taken up refuge there. So, for several days they were beheading the six hundred souls. Both men and women were beheaded indiscriminately, their heads were then buried in the hole under this monolith, and their bodies thrown into this exact patch of icy sea."

Now Javier, lost in his thoughts, looks down at the waves roaring against the rocks, imagining each time they break that they're the open hands reaching out from those headless bodies, begging for their heads back.

"But you know what you're talking about," then comes a man's voice to his left, in perfect Spanish, "all that happened far away from here, from Sitges."

Javier turns toward this man. Then to his right. Elena isn't there.

"Sorry for bothering you . . ." continues the same man, "but when I saw you there . . . talking to yourself . . . I couldn't help but listen to your story—"

"But," Javier cuts him off, "didn't you see a woman our age standing here with me? She has green eyes . . ."

"Sorry, sir," says the other, more serious now. "But you and I are not the same age."

For the umpteenth time today I have taken stock of my situation. For every step I take, I go back two. And so an old and tired Javier, aged sixty-six years, trudges heavily back to his hotel in Sitges. Meanwhile, everything around him breaks. Once he's reached the hotel, he stops for a moment in the doorway. Rooted there stupidly, he looks at the tragicomic image of himself reflected in the door's large glass panes. He sees an old man, tired and alone, waiting for sunset. The evening sun is still at large, illuminating the filth with its yellow light. This yellow light, of this country, his country.

It's light outside, and the terror sets in, Michel Houellebecq once wrote.

Later on, Nacho Vegas included this phrase in a disquieting song.

At last he enters his hotel. At a table in the lobby, a journalist is interviewing someone who appears to be a young writer. They're speaking English. The young man—thin and very well dressed in a classic way verging on old-fashioned—moves his calm, slender hands when he talks. His long hair falls in disarray, and Javier sees that in his gaze there's not just one focus but many—infinite—planes of everything he sees in the lobby of the Port Sitges Resort. Javier thinks that once, at a time that will never come back, he had wanted to be that young foreign writer and have that way of looking at reality. He also thinks of Elena. He's thinking of her in the elevator, when he hears the question that the journalist is asking the young author:

"So how much of the novel is autobiographical?" he asks.

And just as the elevator doors are closing, he hears the other's laconic reply:

"Exactly twenty-seven percent."

Twenty-seven percent of nothing, thinks a sixty-six-year-old Javier, up in his room now, where he's getting ready, in broad daylight, to go to bed and sleep. To sleep and wake up thirty-three years older, at ninety-nine. To sleep and die. Or rather, not wake up.

As he closes his eyes, Javier thinks of Elena, of her standing on the cliff, her intense, green eyes staring at him while the stormy sea looms behind her—inhospitable, threatening, merciless, but at the same time benevolent, compassionate. Javier looks back on it all, in his room at the Port Sitges Resort, waiting for the final darkness. Alone, in the end, like he's always been. Alone, so far from the Irish Sea.

Off to the End of the World:
Considerations about the Literary Calling

SELLING VACUUMS IS a hard job.

Selling vacuums on a ship crossing the ocean is an even harder job. There's no dust.

"But there is humidity, and where there's humidity there's mites," I say through my phony smile, addressing some elderly couple peeking out at me from the doorway of their cabin. But even this isn't good enough to get me a sale.

This job of mine's a rough one. Disheartening, you could say, and I say so now to this blond woman on the deck of this transatlantic cruiser carrying us over the ocean toward the southernmost city in the world. She looks at me from behind her sunglasses, leaning on the railing, in front of the vast surface of water. She looks at me the way you'd look at someone you don't know at all, who walks up to you on a voyage to the end of the world and tells you that his job is disheartening.

"Are you death by any chance?" she says in a foreign accent, and smiles, taking off her sunglasses, and without them on she's the living image of Nastassja Kinski, not the youthful image that springs to mind, of the actress in her most famous roles, but the current one, the beauty-in-its-womanly-plenitude image of Nastassja Kinski.

"Are you Nastassja Kinski?" I ask, ignoring her question, and she smiles and looks at me again, saying nothing.

She doesn't say anything, and so I start to talk instead, on the deck of this transatlantic ship called The New Pequod, cruising under an Argentine flag on the way to Ushuaia, the southernmost city in the world, where everything ends and where everything could perhaps start over again. I tell the woman who looks exactly like Nastassja Kinski that, even though I'm working as a vacuum salesman, my true calling is literature. I tell her I'm writing a book of stories that I plan to try and publish, in the hope that by doing so I'll be able to leave my bleak job as a vacuum salesman. I also tell her that in these stories I'm writing, a few of them at least, I myself put in an appearance as one of the characters, and that, in fiction, as well as being a vacuum salesman, I have the extraordinary ability— owing to complex techniques of an extraterrestrial origin—of bringing the dead back to life.

"As long as they're not too dead," I clarify.

"I mean—the recently deceased," I add.

"Or, to put it another way—the undead dead."

I tell her that this is the particular subject of my story "Amnesic Reminiscences of Christ and the Hitchhiking Girl," which came out in a literary magazine, and because of this, I say, because I included myself as a character who, in fiction, has this incredible gift, I get phone calls in the middle of the night. Because it turns out that people have the ugly custom of dying at such hours. Late, very late at night, and then someone calls me. Some desperate person—a relation, a boyfriend, a wife or husband or mother. And it's very unpleasant, because I have to tell them there's nothing I can do, and then they cry and beg for pity, imploring me to give life back to their son, their wife, their lover . . . etc. Because the thing is, faith turns up in those desperate moments, and they believe, or need to believe, that I can reanimate the dead, and so they call me in the middle of the night.

And as a result, I don't sleep.

As a result, when I do manage to sleep, I have nightmares.

But I can't turn off my cell phone. I have to stay operative twenty-four seven. My bosses at Electrolux demand it of me, they force me to.

Sometimes my boss will call me in the middle of the night from an unknown number, always a different one, to see if I have my phone on.

"Are you there?" my boss asks me in those early morning hours.

"Yes," I answer.

"You never know when someone might have the vital need to buy a vacuum," he says, and hangs up.

"And that's what brings me here, to this cruise ship," I continue telling the woman. "There's no coverage here, in the middle of the ocean. There aren't any late-night calls here. There's no shaky voice here, asking if it's really me, telling me it's found my number in the phone book, asking me, begging me to save someone, raise someone up from the dead. I can sleep here, get some rest before attempting to sell vacuums to the passengers on board this ship. And then, after the dreary workday, I'll finally be able to start writing stories based on things that have happened, or are currently happening to me. Stories like the one that's starting right here, right now."

The woman who so eerily resembles Nastassja Kinski tells me that at one time she never would have believed me, she would have written off everything I've told her as sheer nonsense, if it hadn't been that life, her life—she specifies—has taught her that things like this sometimes happen. And then she asks me, since my calling is literature, if I want to listen to the story of her life, or at least the last few months of her life, which no doubt endow it with what small worth any life can hope to claim. I, of course, say yes, but I also suggest that perhaps it would be better if she told me her story in the bar, over a couple of whiskeys, or, better still, perhaps we could go to my cabin, or hers, where we'd be more comfortable as she tells me her story, about which, if she'll let me, I say, I'll take some notes in my notebook.

She says no, for the time being she'll relate her story right here, on this deck, with the cold Atlantic wind lashing against us, and she'll do so, she says, because she is perfectly aware that I think she's Nastassja Kinski, and knows, just as perfectly, that if given the chance any man would try to sleep with his platonic cinematic sweetheart, who in my case was Nastassja Kinski, but she tells me it would be better if I knew some things first. Some important things.

Some things, such as that she never reads.

Some things, such as that she would never go to bed with a writer.

Some things, such as that she was once married to a writer. A writer obsessed by literature. A writer who never managed to publish a single one of his books. A writer who reached a point where he wanted to be a writer-for-hire, to try and eke out an existence with his calling any way he could. A writer who took a job from someone who called him in the middle of the night to write up a story, which the strange caller dictated to him over the phone. A man who said he just wanted the facts on record, that it was all the same to him whose signature the story carried. He said he renounced any claim to the authorship of what he dictated, the important thing was the facts, and her husband could sign his name to the story, if he wanted to. And the man then began to dictate his suicide. He had managed to pass himself off as dead and get buried alive, and was dictating everything from a coffin underground, awaiting his death. The man was dictating his own suicide from a coffin, where he was slowly running out of oxygen, wearing a mask of Felipe González.

"Just a moment . . ." I say, interrupting her. "Did you say he was wearing a mask of Felipe González?"

"Yes," she answers.

"Right."

She goes on to tell me that it was at that point she understood that her husband was going to let the man kill himself in order to write his story with its morbid ending. And seeing this, she continues, she made a move to grab his cell phone away from him to see if she could try to talk with the man and make him tell her where he was so she could save him from his agonizing death. But her husband screamed at her: no! and pushed her up against the wall. And he told her there wasn't anything or anyone that was going to stop him from writing the perfect story with the perfect ending, a story that went beyond fiction and beyond reality. So she left the house and called every hospital she could think of at the time, asking about a man who had died wearing a mask of Felipe González. And finally, after many phone calls, someone said, yes, there had been a man in a mask of Felipe González there, it was his strange last will. Then more phone calls: to cemeteries, to the police, to her husband in handcuffs after the interrogation, charged with attempted negligent homicide. And that was how she saved him. She'd saved the man who was trying to commit suicide with a mask of Felipe González over his face.

Afterward, the police called her to headquarters and a very tall and skinny agent who seemed as though he would snap in two at any moment, as tall as you, Nastassja says (and I say Natassja because after a certain point we have to call people by the name of whom we wish they were, and I'm at that point now), this tall agent told her that the strange man in the mask of the ex-president was flat out refusing to take it off, and wouldn't stop saying that he was dead and that he needed to find her. Find who? the police asked him over and over again. But he just kept answering, Her, and was growing more upset by the minute. And then the agent asked Nastassja if she was the one the man was talking about. Natassja then looks me straight in the eye and asks if I know how things can get sometimes, when our life is falling apart, and we lie, passing ourselves off as someone else, just to try to live another life, and get away from our own. She asks me if I can understand why she told the agent, yes, she was the one the man wanted.

"Yes, I understand. I understand perfectly," I say, and feel the cold air of the Atlantic against my face; a shiver runs down my spine, and I don't know if it's because of the icy wind or because I sense that this story and this woman will somehow become a part of my life, or at least a part of a story in a book of short stories where I'll fictionalize my life. My life, aboard The New Pequod, heading for the end of the world.

Then she tells me that when she went to see the man in the hospital room where he was recuperating from the aftereffects of his failed suicide attempt, he bounded out of his bed, still wearing that mask of Felipe González over his face, and, no doubt certain that she was the one he was searching for, with tears in his eyes, said to her in a solemn voice:

"Kill them! Kill them all!" and then broke into tears, and cried inconsolably.

And after a pause, so that these last words he'd said to her could take on all the weight solemn words should carry when spoken in the middle of the Atlantic, cruising toward the southernmost city in the world, Nastassja asks me if I want to meet him. If I want to meet the man in the mask, who is waiting for her now in her cabin.

I'm a little slow in answering her, because I'm busy jotting down quick notes in my notebook, in handwriting that's nearly illegible, even for me (this is a new creative technique I've developed, since when I read over the illegible notes I've taken, I'm led to confuse certain words with others, giving rise to surprising twists and turns of direction in my stories), but I finally say no. I'd rather not meet the man in the mask of Felipe González. I say no, adding that her story, far-fetched as it seems, is worth telling, and that I'm going to use it in one of my own stories, in fact, but I don't want to know any more about it, because at the moment it's an open narrative that I can play with in my imagination, and which I hope to bring around, in

my writing it, to a strange ending all my own, which I expect
will be a good one.

So I say no.

And Nastassja Kinski exits the story.

A shame. A real shame.

A shame, because the only thing keeping this ludicrous story
going was the sudden appearance, on board a ship heading for
the end of the world, of the protagonist's erotic idol of the silver
screen, generating a sexual tension between him and the sex
symbol of his youth made flesh in the body of Nastassja, who
now puts her sunglasses back on and walks off across the deck
of The New Pequod as the cold wind whips through her blond
hair.

And so the sexual tension along with the story's interest
come to an end.

It's like in almost every American television series. The only
thing that keeps them going is sexual tension.

It's like many Spanish marriages.

But then, will Nastassja Kinski make another appearance in
this story?

No.

A pity.

So now: change of direction; period, new paragraph. I once
wrote about the importance of the period, new paragraph, the
vital importance of the period, new paragraph in order to close
a paragraph, in order to finalize what was being told and to
begin another, different thing, which has little or nothing to do
with the previous one.

So now I'm going to relate some things here, to write them
in my notebook, in my cabin on this ship. Things such as that
what I truly intend to do is reflect on my literary calling. So
here, on my cabin's small writing desk, I begin to put in order all
the stories that will be part of my future short story collection.
I arrange them according to the logical order of things, or at

least things as I see them: first the present, starting from what's happening here and now, and then the past. The past where everything started, where something gave way inside of me on a remote day when I rang a doorbell and someone, whom I can no longer remember and who, in this story, doesn't matter at all, opened the door. And I automatically started talking very rapidly, the way a person talks when he wants to say as much as possible before a door slams in his face, saying that I had rung his doorbell by chance, picking out his place of residence from among numerous others, and was he ever in luck that I had rung precisely at his house, to offer him a technological marvel of a cleaning gadget: an Electrolux vacuum, which isn't merely a vacuum, but also cleanliness itself and a peaceful home, a true breakthrough in the vacuum arena . . .

And then:

Buuuuuuuuuuuuuuuuuuzzzzzzzzzzzzzzz.

And a blinding light.

And a lot of noise. And I was about to tell whoever it was that it seemed pretty noisy inside his house, and that there must be quite a lot of people in there making a big mess, and that he really seemed in sore need of a vacuum. But then I realized that the noise was in my head. A deafening noise.

A deafening noise of enormous waves crashing against a cliff.

Then all of a sudden—silence—and I had a vision of a sea, huge, dark, and threatening, but intoxicating at the same time, and sublimely beautiful, and it felt like a part of me, it was calling me; I thought then of throwing myself into it and sinking down through its unfathomable waters, down to the furthest depth, in a descent that I imagined as an ovarian descent, to the most intimate, to the primeval, to the end and the beginning of everything. But, in my vision, something made me take a few steps back, away from the abyss, with my hand stretched out behind me; then my fingers brushed against hers, and as I turned around I saw her deep green eyes looking back at me.

Her. Her white skin and her green eyes and her silence and that sea, which I then knew, without knowing how, but with absolute certainty, was the Irish Sea.

And then I had the urge to put that silence in writing. A silence like a blank sheet of paper filling up with the terrible and swift and dangerous words that surge up from automatic writing. I wanted to describe that sea and that silence and her.

This woman, this silence, and the Irish Sea behind it all.

And that was the beginning of everything. I admit it here. Closing in on Ushuaia, the southernmost city in the world, where everything ends only to start all over again.

So here I am, at the beginning's end. It's all been written. It's all in this fistful of stories I'm putting in order, which I'll call: *The Irish Sea.* I arrange them by placing at the front the stories that tell what's happening, followed by what's just happened, and then what was, until it comes around at last to the absolute beginning, the seed of it all, the:

Buuuuuuuuuuuuuuuuuuuuzzzzzzzzzzzzzzzzz.

And then, directly after this, the Irish Sea.

And at the beginning of the book, on the very first page, I write:

These stories are a product of the author's imagination. Any similarity of the situations or characters in this book with real-life persons or events is pure and involuntary coincidence.

Then I write:

Ha!

Ha! Ha! Ha!

And I slip these pages that form the first draft of a book entitled *The Irish Sea* into the desk drawer. Because someone's knocking on the door of my cabin. I open it and there she is: Nastassja.

Her, again. That's the way things are: sometimes I'm wrong, sometimes I lie, sometimes I lie and I'm wrong at the same time. There she is, asking me if she can come in; I say yes, and ask her where the man with the mask of Felipe González is. She says he's gone down to land, seeing as we've arrived at Ushuaia, to which I say, no, that's impossible, how could we have arrived without my noticing. Nastassja says it is possible, and that we'd entered the Beagle Channel hours ago and are now sitting in the Ushuaia port, and that she's gone down to land, too, and walked around the small town, down its main street lined with small colorful houses lashed by the eternal wind of the end of the world, with him, the man in the mask of Felipe González, and that they'd wandered around some and left the small settlement behind, following a deserted road that ran through a field, which was where they saw her, a sight that had stopped the masked man dead in his tracks, but then he'd walked up to her, and looked her in the eyes, and told her he understood, he knew her pain. And now he's with her.

"Her? Her who?" I ask without understanding a thing.

"The naked woman who was kneeling in the grass like she was praying."

"What? A naked woman kneeling in the grass?" I repeat.

She looks at me and doesn't say anything. She stares straight at me with her eyes wide open and vibrantly green for a long time, and then I remember that Nastassja Kinski, the actress, doesn't have green eyes, and I know then that what she's been telling me is a lie, it's all a lie—there wasn't any naked woman kneeling in the grass, we haven't arrived at Ushuaia yet, everything I've been told by this woman, who oddly enough, as it happens, I now realize doesn't actually look much like the movie actress, is a lie. It's a lie that she'd been with the man in the mask, because such a man simply doesn't exist, he is merely a character from one of my stories, and I also know that she was never married to a hack writer, because he's yet another one of my characters. And then I, too, stop telling myself lies. I stop, because deep down I know Ushuaia doesn't really exist. Ushuaia is only a patriotic Argentine invention, created so that Argentina could preen itself for having the southernmost city in the world, the city of the world's end and beginning. It's just a fistful of photographs, perhaps shot one gusty and overcast day against the backdrop of some Californian beach, by a Los Angeles advertising firm hired by the Argentine government. And so I know this ship, The New Pequod, under pretext of horrible storms or hurricane winds, will never arrive at its destination, and that we'll turn back with the ephemeral happiness of, yes, having almost made it.

But then why has she told me all this? How does she know everything?

Buuuuuuuuuuuuuuuuuuzzzzzzzzzzzzzzzzzz (once again).

I understand.

Now I understand everything.

That's not how it was.

I was wrong.

It's she. Nastassja is she. She knows everything, from the beginning. She was there, with the Irish Sea in the background, and the beginning of everything. She is the woman from my vision. She is the reason I write. She has told me all this so I'll write this story.

And I walk up to her and touch her face, and tell her I've missed her very much, that sometimes I even thought she didn't exist and was only a part of my imagination, and I say many other things as well, not knowing if they're understood, because I don't say them to anybody, I say them to myself, like an inconsolable prayer, like crying, like crying from fulfillment, like the automatic writing of a madman, that's it: a madman, because I couldn't be anything else. And she tells me she's here, it's true, all the rest doesn't matter, and kisses me with sea-dampened lips, and I tell her, with tears in my eyes, that I must write all this, that I need to, and she says that I must do it, I have to.

Here, heading for Ushuaia, the world's southernmost ghost

town, where everything ends and where everything begins.

Once again.

And her last words resound in my head and I turn to her and she's looking at me, and I feel that now everything in my life, whatever may come, will have to be different. A man must follow his calling. Take a risk, commit.

In this moment, I decide. I make the biggest decision of my life.

There was no need.

My cell phone rings and a number with an outlandish prefix code appears on the screen. But how could it be? I say to myself, there's no coverage here in the middle of the ocean. I answer it, and a voice with the thick alien accent of the planet Lux tells me:

"You're fired."

II. Autobiography of Someone Else

Autobiography of Someone Else

1.

ON THE MORNING that Jorge decides to leave his wife it's very bright out. A hard, yellow light. Each detail is stripped bare by this light, each imperfection. It shows the filth, the scratches in the surfaces of things.

It's November and he's just got back from a long trip. He'd been traveling the whole night. She sleeps while he makes coffee. He sits down at the living room table, waiting as he drinks black coffee. By nine in the morning she still hasn't woken up—it's Sunday, and she usually gets up late, the morning already well advanced. So he writes her a long note. A note in which no reasons or motives are given, only nebulous feelings. He tries to describe this light, too, which illuminates everything, but he can't, all that comes of it is a vague attempt. He explains this as well. Then he writes that he's truly sorry, that it's all his fault, that she wasn't to blame, just him, and that the time had come for him to go. To flee. Flee, and perhaps kill himself. He doesn't write this last part, just thinks it. He sits there, motionless, until he can't take it anymore and bursts into tears. Bursts into tears that run freely down his face, and flees, from pain, from himself.

He flees. And some lines of Robert Walser's make it so he doesn't kill himself.

Today I walked through the mountains. The weather was damp, and the entire region was gray. But the road was soft and in places very clean. At first I had my coat on; soon, however, I pulled it off, folded it together, and laid it upon my arm, Walser began.

He walks through the mountains. The weather is damp, and the entire region is gray. But the road is soft and in places very clean. At first he has his coat on; soon, however, he pulls it off, folds it together, and lays it upon his arm. He walks a little farther up the trail until he gets back to the overlook off the highway that runs through the Despeñaperros Pass. Taking one last look, he imagines it's not he who looks, but that he's looking out from eyes other than his own. He feels insignificant and incapable of forming any opinion of what he sees. Now the abyss is opening up at his feet and he imagines, without knowing why, that the cold air is a tongue. A damp tongue. That of an old woman who is slowly dying. And the damp, cold tongue of an elderly, cold woman who is slowly dying laps his face.

He looks into the abyss and thinks of Robert Walser. He thinks of his way of telling a story, where the narrator slowly becomes insignificant until, in the end, he disappears. He thinks of Walser, of all the critics and publishers who tried to force him to be like Hermann Hesse. He thinks of Walser hating Hesse, his wisdom, his saintliness. Jorge considers all these things about the writer of the lowlands. And that's how he feels, like that insignificant Walserian figure who starts out by gradually losing his capacity for action, and, in the end, for being. And so Jorge stares into the abyss, not seeing it with his own eyes, however, because by now, gazing downward, he's disappeared.

He guides his car without any more pit stops along endless miles of northbound highway. Because, contrary to Herman Hesse, who once said the only flight possible is always southward, Jorge is fleeing to the north. He needs to escape from that yellow light. This yellow light that lays bare all the squalor surrounding him, as it reveals that everything it touches is marred.

After many long hours of driving he arrives at his destination, there in the north. It's a rainy gray evening as he approaches the ancient City of Stone. He's come to this place of ten years ago where it all began, and he's come back now to dig up the root of what was. He takes the last exit into the city from the northwest highway. He likes that view of the City of Stone folded into itself by the slow river, the view of the old bridge, and of the iron bridge where only trains chug past, and suicides who throw themselves from the steel tracks on cloudy days like this one. And there's the new bridge as well, with its white, piercing modernity and its bizarre pedestrian footbridge tracing a fantastic eight at a great height over the road where automobiles cross above the river, which courses even farther below, slow and forgotten, with the slowness and oblivion of the eternal. The new bridge: future meeting place, no doubt, of the ancient City of Stone's coming generations of suicides.

He's reserved a room in the Hotel San Martín, an old monolith near the beautiful Parque de San Lázaro in the city center, a vestige of glorious, industrial times, when the Citroën factory and the booming textile and wine industries brought a never-before-seen prosperity to the City of Stone. He stays in his room, situated on one of the building's upper floors. But rather than unpack his suitcase, he spends a long time gazing out of the large window at the enormous old black trees of the Parque de San Lázaro, the cathedral that's hinted at to its right behind the buildings that line the Paseo, the blue pigeons seeking shelter from the fine rain, and behind all this the mountain, also blue, now sinking into black, in the background. The blue-black mountain, disappearing, with the night, behind the glass, which slowly, very slowly, shows back his own reflection.

And when all he can see is his mirrored image, finding this unbearable, he lies back on the bed, opens a small notebook with gray covers and starts to write. He writes about his life, about his memories, which course slowly, windingly over the immaculate white of the paper.

After some time, Jorge stops writing, gets up and goes over to the window, feeling dizzy. Undoing the safety catch, he throws open the window, and as the cold air rushes into his face he feels the temptation of ceasing to exist. This thought gives way to another, more abstract and disjointed, in which he sees his own body falling faster and faster into an abyss, and the fear this inspires in him turns quickly to panic. It's the second time in just a few days that he's seriously considered the possibility of committing suicide. He turns around and hurries over to his suitcase, which is still lying unpacked on the floor. He rummages for the small box in one of the side pockets and pops an Orfidal. And then another. He tries to wait, but he can't and takes a third. He lies down on the bed and forces his eyes shut. And it's strange, but the last thing he hears before he falls asleep is what sounds like a howling wolf, although it's more likely a dog, or perhaps it's just a man out on the railway tracks of the iron bridge, only a short way off.

Jorge dreams of his son, far away from him now, and of his children's future children, and then of a long highway, extraordinarily long, that perhaps doesn't lead anywhere, but that he must take since he knows he has to leave; to leave immediately, that's the goal.

Jorge has woken up around noon. He has drunk the better part of the mini-bar's contents. He's aware that he hasn't eaten anything in two days, but he doesn't feel hungry at all. He keeps drinking all afternoon, pacing himself in order not to finish all the alcohol too soon. Drinking slowly, and from time to time writing in his gray notebook, or looking out of the large window at the City of Stone below him.

Finally, he decides to go out. First, he takes a long, hot shower. Then he puts on clean clothes and goes down. The smell of the City of Stone is unmistakable, the hue of the stones, of the walls, their textures, it all brings him back to ten years ago. He senses the gray, oppressive sky above him and begins to feel a sort of agoraphobia. He goes into the first bar he finds. It's a small, elongated room where there are only two or three men drinking beneath a weak light. He orders a whiskey from the overweight bartender. He drains it in three swallows and orders another. He starts to calm down. He concentrates on his breathing and takes his small notebook from his coat pocket and rereads what he's written. He finishes what's left of the whiskey in his glass. He orders a third and, as he orders it, tells the bartender, encouraged no doubt by the alcohol, that the bar reminds him a great deal of another one just like it, a bar in the Cíes Islands, he thinks. He also asks the bartender if he wants to hear some autobiographical fragments he's written, in the gray notebook that he's just set down on the bar, as it happens, which take place on the island of San Martiño, in the Cíes, where one winter he'd gone into a bar exactly like this one, he now makes clear, where the men sat hunched over the bar and drank as if they'd just become aware of the banality of their lives.

"It sure must be a long story," the fat bartender says, glancing up at him with tired eyes beneath which the drooping skin forms two enormous bags.

"Sure must," he agrees.

"And I don't doubt this story of yours must be one hell of an unbelievable story. Matter of fact," continues the bartender, "just as unbelievable as there being a bar just like this one in the Cíes Islands."

His voice is raspy, and it breaks a little at the end of his last comment. Jorge takes a sip from his glass and looks at the fat bartender. Waiting. After a few seconds, the bartender says:

"There isn't any bar like this in San Martiño, because they don't have anything over there. And when it's winter in the Cíes Islands, no one's there." And these last three words he says leaving long pauses between each one.

"In winter, no one's there," he repeats.

"I have a lot of imagination," Jorge says.

"No. You're a liar," the other responds.

Now, Jorge, the man with the gray notebook, stares without expressing any kind of emotion whatsoever at the exhausted eyes of the fat bartender, under which sag bags of skin that seem to carry the weight of the world. He holds the defiant stare until the other man lowers his eyes and, taking the money that Jorge has put down on the bar, moves off heavily toward the cash register.

Jorge leaves the bar and breathes in the nocturnal air of the ancient City of Stone. He walks through San Lázaro Park by night, under the branches of the immense dark trees. He takes Calle Santo Domingo to the Plaza of Iron. Hardly anyone else is outside walking on this cold autumn night. He hears steps of heels on the cobblestones getting nearer. He turns toward the sound. It's a woman who asks him for a light. He tells her he's sorry, but he doesn't smoke. This is a lie, and he considers why he answered that way as he continues walking.

A light rain starts to fall, slowly soaking his coat and hair. He is near the Café Latino. He speeds up his pace, continuing at a light jog until he arrives at the door. He goes inside. The atmosphere is agreeable. He takes off his coat and hangs it on the rack. There aren't too many people around. It's late for a Wednesday, and it's November. He always liked this café and it hasn't changed at all. It's just as he remembered it. The hardwood floors and the circular wrought-iron tables with the marble tops. The high ceiling and the wooden stairs that climb up to a second level perched on a few columns. Beneath these the light is dim and instead of chairs the tables stand by either armchairs or couches of a dyed-green leather so dark it looks black. He chooses a table in this more private and less illuminated part of the café. Having settled into an armchair, he orders his fourth whiskey of the night.

He opens his notebook back up. But as he's about to start writing, he looks up and sees a young woman sitting a few tables away, reading. She's young. Much younger than she seems to him at first. But then, as he looks closer, he notices the lines at the corners of her eyes and thinks maybe she could be his age, or a few years younger. He wonders how he didn't notice her when he came in, since he must have walked right by her to get to where he's now sitting. He pretends to read what he's written in the notebook as he observes her. Her skin is pale and she has long black hair that's gathered up at the back of her neck, her eyes seem, or he imagines them to be, light-colored, of an indefinite shade. But the thing about the woman that Jorge finds most attractive is that in her hands she's holding a book entitled: *The Walk*, by Robert Walser.

At last, Jorge gets up from his seat and heads over to where the woman is. Drawing up next to her, he says, paraphrasing Walser in the beginning of this book:

"I have to report that, I no longer know at exactly what time, I left my writing room, or room of spirits, and went down the stairs to go out, and I've arrived right here."

She looks up at him, at first in surprise, but then a smile spreads across her face, and she invites him to sit down with her.

"My name's Isabel," she says, and seeing her up close, Jorge understands it's not that the woman is older than he is, the problem is that she's sick. Her pale skin has a dull grayish tinge to it, and her eyes seem as tired as the ancient City of Stone in which she and Jorge have crossed paths.

"Jorge," he says, and then adds as a joke, "Jorge Walser," and she smiles again and talks to him about the book she's reading and about those words that seem to bear the mark of an attempt to hide the disquiet present in the deepest, smallest, and most insignificant things. She confesses, then, that she had noticed him also, and that she had seen how he was watching her, and she says that although she didn't find him handsome, there was one thing she had liked about him ever since he first slinked into the café, even before he had become aware of her presence and begun to observe her, and it was this: his elegance. The elegance of practicing the timid art of going unnoticed. He tells her he could teach her something he's learned from reading Walser.

"What? The art of learning to live?" she asks.

"No, the art of disappearing," he answers. And hearing this, she lapses into a long silence, staring at him without blinking. He looks back at her and they stay like this until he asks her if she will go with him to the Cíes Islands tomorrow to disappear. She says yes, she'll go to the Cíes Islands with him and they'll disappear together. Then Jorge asks her if she's married or living with anyone. Her look is serious as she stares into his eyes and answers:

"You shouldn't ask someone who's trying to disappear about their life."

They leave the café together, pressing close to one another as the light rain falls on them as far as the Hotel San Martín. They go up to the room, where they look at each other and touch each other's face and hair for a long time, until they begin to shiver and become aware of the soaked clothes sticking to their bodies. They undress and continue to caress each other. They look at each other's body, wasted away by sickness and time. Isabel's extreme thinness gives Jorge a jolt. They embrace and kiss, and each of them sinks, while at the same time seeking refuge from their own pain, into the pain of the other.

2.

They cover the barely sixty miles between the City of Stone and Vigo in Jorge's car. During the trip both Isabel and Jorge remain in a silence that they interrupt only to make simple comments on the heavy gray clouds blanketing the sky. At one point, paraphrasing something which Enrique Vila-Matas will write in the future, Jorge says: this gray sky above us, this whole landscape, has the beauty of a northern blues, if such a thing as a northern blues could exist.

They arrive at Vigo, where finding a ship willing to take them to the Cíes in November proves difficult. Everywhere they go and ask they're informed that the maritime routes are only open till September. Finally, Isabel makes a few calls on her cell phone and they find a Portuguese man who owns a small boat and offers to take them for a small sum. The Portuguese man, who strangely reminds Jorge of the fat, tired-eyed bartender from the dive in the City of Stone, barely says a word to them, and doesn't even give them his name.

The sea looks like a living, breathing creature, and its calm seems to Jorge like the calm before the storm. The fat Portuguese man is in the back handling the motor and murmuring a few words in his language that sound like curses as he looks up at the gray storm clouds overhead. Isabel is in the prow, the wind blowing through her black hair as the sea sprays up and wets her clothes, but it doesn't seem to bother her. Jorge watches the way she seems to be challenging the sea, and not just this, but something else within her thoughts, maybe the sickness weakening her body, facing it, summoning it up like a demon.

As they're putting in at the pier, a lightning bolt flashes across the sky, which has gone from gray to almost black. They get down from the ship as the Portuguese man swears and spits into the water. Jorge helps Isabel down, giving her his hand; he feels the warm touch of her skin and notices the way her hand firmly grips his and, for some reason, Jorge thinks of a paw. The paw of a sick animal. One whose master helps it up in order to compassionately point his gun at it, and put an end in one shot to its suffering and its life.

They climb the road leading away from the pier, and looking back they see the fat Portuguese man—his tired eyes and the enormous bags of skin beneath them that seem to carry the weight of the world. The Portuguese man, for his part, watches them go, looking as though he's chewing something. Neither Jorge nor Isabel is completely certain that he'll wait for them for very long.

They take the road that leads up into the cliffs. It's a difficult climb, and they have to take hold of tree roots and weeds to keep going. After a few minutes' progress, her weakened body no doubt exhausted from all the activity, Isabel, who's a few yards behind Jorge, asks in a strained voice:

"And what will we do to disappear?"

And what will we do to disappear? Maurice Blanchot once wrote.

And hearing Isabel's strained voice, Jorge feels guilty for having made her climb this craggy trail given her physical weakness. He turns around to where she is. But no one's there. He shouts her name.

"Isabel!" And the cliffs answer back with the echo of his own voice.

No one's there.

And then there come to his mind the words of the fat bartender who looked so much like—exactly like, he thinks now—the Portuguese man with the small boat.

"No one's there," the bartender had said, dragging out the pauses between each word.

. . . then he experienced a feeling of extraordinary lightness, a kind of beatitude (nothing happy, however), sovereign elation? The encounter of death with death? Perhaps he was suddenly invincible. Dead-immortal. Perhaps ecstasy. Or rather the feeling of compassion for suffering humanity, the joy of not being immortal or eternal, wrote Maurice Blanchot.

And then he tosses into the cliffs abyss the gray notebook where he's written the autobiography of someone else.

Someone else who he's not.

And then Jorge Walser prepares to disappear.

Two Hundred Naked Women Kneeling in a Green Wisconsin Prairie: A Matter of Faith

TWO HUNDRED NAKED women kneeling in a green Wisconsin prairie.

Yes, that was the photograph, and yes, that's how it all started. The picture was taken with a powerful telephoto lens in a no doubt restricted area somewhere in Wisconsin, and published in a local newspaper of a small city in Buffalo County. The item was then picked up by various international papers.

In the end, a government mouthpiece had a few things to explain at a tumultuous press conference. Some shameful things, depending on how you look at it.

That's why I'm here, at this hotel in this quaint little city in Wisconsin. Here I am, gazing at the reflection of my own aged face in the bathroom mirror.

"The fact that neurons lack the ability to self-reproduce is a favorable one, because that way our essential 'I' never changes," the scientist says over the radio I've switched on in my room.

Ha!

Ha! Ha!

Then why am I reciting these solemn axioms to myself in front of the mirror? These phrases that bring my life crashing down.

God does not exist.

I feel an uncontainable desire for Vina.

I'm a vegetarian.

I wasn't that way before, before God ceased existing for me, before I felt this brutal attraction to a woman, before I gave up eating meat once and for all. Am I still myself?

Myself, Father Sebastiano Lamborbo. Myself, hunter of saints, watchman of the Holy Father. Myself, emissary of the Church, sent to this small city in Wisconsin to evaluate on site these ethical questions, and draw up the pertinent report.

The one regarding the two hundred naked women kneeling in a field, and all that.

Sometimes it happens.

It's not that strange, it's only that, sometimes, you can't see the forest for the trees.

Or the cows for the trees.

(Details below.)

But now, let's leave that story behind and move on to the story buried under the story, to the great iceberg under water, from which only the tip pokes out, let's move on to the submerged part, to what destroyed the hull of the indestructible *Titanic*, and my life, to that enormous submerged iceberg.

Which made everyone think Kate Winslet was a good actress.

She was nominated for an Oscar on account of that movie.

Then they gave it to her for her performance in *The Reader*.

Then she married some guy named Ned Rocknroll. Ned Rocknroll?

It's no coincidence that I'm saying all this now, because I say all this to Freaky Frank, the author of the photographs of the two hundred women kneeling naked in a green field, the writer who has stopped writing because—he argues—there aren't any more stories, it's all been said. So I tell him he should write about Kate Winslet, that there's a good story in it, and he should stop roaming around the prairies of Wisconsin taking pornographic photographs that end up complicating the lives of so many people.

People like me.

Because if those photographs didn't exist, I wouldn't have

met Vina and I wouldn't have stopped believing in God, and I wouldn't have become a vegetarian.

But let's move on to my personal iceberg.

Let's move on to Vina.

Vina, dancing half-naked on the bed in my hotel room, to the rhythm of her mix CD. Dancing to a remix of "Brown Sugar" by the Stones. And I, at the moment, don't believe in God, or at least in the superior, omnipotent God who orders the world's chaos, not in that kind of God, because I, for the time being, am totally in thrall to the earthliest desire. But the music changes, it grows more melodic and the movements of Vina's body adapt perfectly to the tune and the dramatic, at times eerie, voice of Lana del Rey, who says something like this: Come and take me to the wild side / Let me kiss you hard in the pouring rain / You like your girls insane / Choose your last words / This is the last time / Because we're born to die.

And then the last rays of sun shoot in through the window and everything takes on a reddish hue and the calm of things impresses itself on my senses and I open the window and the fresh and sad air blows in, and I . . . believe in God.

I believe in God, in his work, in my duty.

And Vina touches my back and hits stop on the CD player and the music stops and I turn around and her face is inches from mine and her deep green eyes look at me and she brings her lips to mine and kisses me and . . . I don't believe in God anymore.

Stop: now I don't believe.

Play: now I believe.

Now, I don't believe.

Now, I believe.

And now I rewind.

And I cover my ears, because the sharp sound grates on my nerves.

Play.

"Sometimes you can't see the forest for the trees," Freaky Frank is saying, the writer who no longer writes, the author of the photos, the sender, not so anonymous now, but who wanted to be, of that packet of photographs mailed off to a local newspaper in this small city called Alma, where I, Father Sebastiano Lamborbo, have stopped believing in God.

I came to Alma and stopped believing in God. How do you like that?

I also became a vegetarian here, but this was because of the business with the women. You know, the two hundred naked women kneeling in a green Wisconsin prairie. Everybody knows.

It was on TV.

That's why I'm here. But it would be better if I explained myself, some people don't watch TV.

At first, it was believed to be a sect, you know, the kind that crops up in the American prairies, goes out on sunny days, in the nude, to pray and then drink a death-cocktail: a little orange juice, vodka, crushed ice, and a splash of cyanide, and wait with their backpacks packed and their glossy Nike sports shoes for their extraterrestrial gods to come for them, and whisk them away to the planet Lux, for example.

But that wasn't it.

They were cows.

"What? Cows?" I ask Freaky Frank, the writer who's given up writing, and who's been newly appointed as my personal assistant and chief of the federal investigation committee, and he shows me his report, which consists of several pages from Wikipedia that he hasn't even bothered to cut and paste, merely printed out as is from the website.

I'm flipping through the reports on U.S. cattle production and genetic improvements introduced into the breeding and use of livestock.

This all started, Freaky Frank begins to relate in a grave tone, at a conference initiated by the State Institute for Competitive Business, which gathered together livestock concerns and a number of genetic research and development companies. The main question was to look for a substantial improvement in the breeding and use of both the milk breeds and those intended for meat. The first few meetings that were held saw no shortage of proposals, but—whether it was for the high costs, as the cattle-breeders suggested, or for the impossibility or complexity of certain genetic processes—they were always rejected. Things seemed to be at a standstill, when a rancher from the Midwest shouted from the middle of the auditorium:

"And why don't we breed a cow in the shape of a woman!"

A hush fell over the room, but then someone remarked that this would be a livestock revolution, an unprecedented revaluation of the United States cattle market, and then a couple of genetic engineers said that after a long process of selection, cross-breeding, and genetic modification, it wouldn't be so wild to think they could pull it off.

"What's more," the president and top shareholder of one of the northern California livestock companies said at this point, "I'm prepared to invest a large sum of money in this project."

Then they all set about calculating the appropriate funds for the different directors of United States food safety, making another entry, and it was substantial, for certain higher-ups at the World Health Organization. And once that was sorted out, they found themselves a farm in a more or less out-of-the-way and inaccessible location, several miles from the small city of Alma, in Wisconsin.

"So that God will be with us," pronounced the livestock entrepreneur from the Midwest.

And then the photographs came out, developed by Freaky Frank and sent to a local newspaper, after which, the global circulation and the scandal, and that's why I'm here.

I'm the Vatican's emissary. The investigation committee. The one who writes the report so that God may take a position on the matter.

And no, I haven't tried either the meat or the milk of this new breed of cows.

I'm a vegetarian.

I have, however, seen them up close, grazing among the trees in the green fields of Wisconsin. And yes, they resembled two hundred nude women down on their knees, praying.

I have also attended their slaughter and seen the sanitary controls and I have studied the nutritional reports of their meat and milk. All I can say is that they're cows that are shaped like women. I think about writing this in my report, but something keeps me from doing so, or at least from leaving it at that. I look over one of the reports in front of me now, which was drawn up by the correspondent from the FAO: Scientific investigation has demonstrated that warm-blooded animals— including livestock—feel pain and fear. Mammals in particular, including those intended for food production, have a cerebral structure that permits them to feel fright and pain, and it is quite probable that they experience pain in the same way that humans do. Fear and pain are very significant causes of stress in livestock, and stress affects the quality of the meat. Pain is generally the consequence of an injury or of maltreatment, and may be alleviated by this new breed of cows, which, owing to their resemblance to human individuals of the female sex, will generate in their caretakers a certain empathy, perhaps unconscious, as fellow beings, therefore ensuring the proper care and management of livestock in an expert and efficient manner, utilizing the appropriate facilities and measures to assure their well-being, which will prevent deficiencies in the quality of their meat and other derived products.

And now a naked woman approaches me, she stops a few yards off. Her skin is fair, perhaps it looks a little more fatty than normal, perhaps her maxillaries seem a little more developed than they should be, but her dark eyes don't seem to be at all different from a human being's. She gazes back at me for a few seconds, then kneels down on the grass, as if she were praying, and begins to chew grass.

I don't want to think of anything else, I just want to forget everything for a while, or perhaps, why not, to believe that she's just a naked woman who's gone insane, and is praying on the grass.

Maybe she is.

Maybe that's all she is. A naked woman, praying on the grass, who has looked over at me, and I feel there's something in those eyes, an enormous pain, deep, measureless, and ancient, I feel as if there isn't anything or anyone else around, as if, for example, I were at the end of the world, or perhaps in a field, facing this woman, in the outskirts of the world's southernmost city, Ushuaia, where everything ends and where everything begins.

Maybe this is the only thing that's certain and the rest is just a madman's soliloquy. A number of pages written by a nutcase.

Maybe it's about time I left, went back home.

Went back home without seeing Vina again, without even calling her.

Maybe go back to believing in God.

Sometimes.

Now I believe.

Now I don't.

Now I believe.

We're born to die, and, no doubt, we also believe to die.

It's easier that way.

The Raft of the Medusa

1.

W HEN THE CREATIVE writing group set themselves the task of writing something that would take as its point of departure Theodore Géricault's painting *The Raft of the Medusa*, which shows a raft adrift with several emaciated castaways who've sighted a ship in the distance, Samuel thought of writing a symbolic story parallel to the real one which had inspired the painting. The real story took place when the French frigate Méduse shipwrecked off the coast of Mauritania, and part of its crew hurriedly built a raft to try to reach the coast. From that point on, a number of horrendous events befell the one hundred and forty-seven people left adrift on the raft: hunger, thirst, suicides, murders, madness, and even cannibalism; only fifteen of the shipwrecked sailors surviving. Samuel thought of writing a story based on the same feelings and sensations as those poor bastards had. He thought of writing a story parallel to the real one, a story of anguish, suffering, and a timid hope, bathed in the same white, almost unreal light as in the painting.

Samuel thinks of how he has never found himself in such dire straits, nor could he imagine himself in such a situation, and he doesn't like to write about what he doesn't know. He clearly remembers thinking about all this that evening. He was in the living room. He stood staring at the leather sofa and at the white wall, taking long gulps of a non-alcoholic beer. Then he remembered Armando. Samuel was to go on a work-related trip soon to Santiago de Compostela. He was going to take his car, which, as anyone knows, is ludicrous: to drive from Almería to Santiago; but his fear of flying had got the better of him. Because of this, he thought he would only have to go a few miles out of his way during the trip to get to Vigo, where he could talk with Armando. Armando was an acquaintance of his. An old client with whom, out of friendship, he still kept up a certain contact. Armando was a sailing enthusiast and he had once told Samuel (this was some six years ago) that during one passage he had suffered a shipwreck off the coasts of the Cíes Islands.

Samuel wrote him an e-mail in which he explained all this. He told him about the painting *The Raft of the Medusa*, about the creative writing workshop and about the story he had to compose based on the painting. In the subject field of the e-mail, he wrote: Sometimes strange things happen to me.

He spent that evening pacing from one end of the house to the other, with nothing to do. Anyway, ever since Sofia, his wife, had left him, he'd felt like he had nothing to do. Hardly a year after their marriage, she had left him and gone to Honduras.

"Honduras? Why the hell are you going to Honduras?" Samuel remembers he said. Of course, she didn't go to Honduras alone, but with her lover: a Honduran actor who had work as Brad Pitt's stunt double. Samuel remembers very well when he'd wanted, despite her protests, to accompany her to the airport and saw him there. He didn't look anything like Brad Pitt.

"You don't look anything like Brad Pitt," he'd spat at him.

"It doesn't really matter," the other had said in a calm voice. "Everyone wants the star to have a dramatic death. When people are shooting at me, or I'm plummeting to the ground, everyone wants me to be him, Brad, everyone wants to see him die. They see me as him because they deeply want it to be him."

The non-alcoholic beers gave way to others with alcohol in them, and these to a couple of gin and tonics. So he was fairly drunk when he read Armando's e-mail responding to his own.

"I'm going to be away from Vigo as of tomorrow. I'm taking a few days off to go sailing. Quite a coincidence, isn't it! You bring up that shipwreck and tomorrow I'm going sailing . . . Anyway, I don't think we'll be able to see each other, unless you head out from Almería right now in your car, which you aren't about to do. But don't worry, as soon as I get back I'll write you an e-mail and fill you in on the whole thing. It was horrible, Isolda and I thought we were going to die," Armando wrote.

Samuel wrote back immediately. He could barely make out the letters on the keyboard.

"Isolda? Isolda who? You told me you were alone . . ."

He had been staring at the screen for an hour. Waiting, drunk, an empty glass in his hand, when a new e-mail from Armando appeared in the inbox:

"I didn't mention it to anyone back then, now, after my divorce, I can talk about it. It all happened six years ago, I wasn't alone in the sailboat. There was a woman with me. Her name was Isolda."

Again, Samuel wrote anxiously:

"Her last name. What was her last name?"

After just a few seconds Armando's message came up:

"Marques. Her name's Isolda Marques and now she's my wife. You're being very odd, Samuel."

Samuel thought that sometimes strange things happened to him, which became too complicated. Six years ago, he'd slept with Isolda Marques.

He picked up the hard copy of the painting he'd printed out and stared at it. He saw himself as one of those castaways: failed, hopeless, ground down by life and circumstance. He thought of his failure, of the sentimental failure of his life, and then Samuel thought that he himself had to get to the bottom of this failure, to its causes and ultimate consequences, he had to understand it, comprehend his failure, he had to see Armando and Isolda, because there, he suspected, was the seed of his failure, in that shipwreck off the coasts of the Cíes Islands.

He drank four cups of coffee, got in his Ford, and left in the dark of night for Vigo under a torrential rain. It never rains in Almería, but now the universal deluge was coming down. Strange things were running their course. The consequences would be unpredictable.

In the downpour, going only fifty miles an hour, Samuel thought about what he'd read of the terrible event. There came to his mind a sentence that the critic Jonathan Miles had written in an article for *The Times*: the raft carried the survivors to the frontiers of human experience. Crazed, parched, and starved, they slaughtered mutineers, ate their dead companions and killed the weakest. Samuel thought about this, and talking out loud to himself he said, "I'm going to the frontiers of human experience." And then, without knowing why, in his mind he related this sentence to the novel *Journey to the End of the Night*, by Céline. Then he thought of how the French were to blame for everything: those damned French always ended up complicating his life. He remembered, then, the deep impression that Houellebecq's *The Possibility of an Island* had made on him, and how it had left him emotionally drained. So maybe he was undertaking a journey parallel to those crazed French castaways on the raft of the Medusa. A journey, no doubt, in the darkness under a strange torrential rain toward the frontiers of human experience up to the end of the night. Damn French, he said to himself, and then he smiled in silence, as the raindrops crashed against the windshield, remembering a sentence of Schopenhauer's: Other parts of the world have monkeys, but Europe has Frenchmen: one thing compensates for the other.

No doubt, in the demented darkness, under the relentless rain, traveling toward the frontiers of human experience up to the ultimate end of his failure, one thing compensated for the other.

2.

Fernando Pessoa wrote *The Book of Disquiet* under the heteronym of Bernardo Soares, out of fragments of a diary, loose reflections, which were found after his death in a state of total disarray and later on brought together in that book. All those notes make up the autobiography of Bernardo Soares. And so Samuel, in a roadside bar at three in the morning, thought that he himself would write *The Book of Failure* with notes that he would cull from that gray notebook resting on the filthy counter of the bar. And he too would use a heteronym to write it. This would be Brad Pitt's true double, the actor who resembled Brad Pitt in every way, but who had resigned himself to failure when he saw how another—who looked nothing like the real Brad Pitt—had taken over his role as Pitt's double, and even made a conquest of his own wife, throwing him into the lowest depths of despair and failure.

Samuel wrote the first lines of *The Book of Failure* in his gray notebook, right there, in front of a cup of cold coffee, in that dirty roadside bar.

"You wouldn't happen to be from Honduras?" he asked the fat South American woman tending bar as he signaled for the bill.

She stared hard at him in complete silence. Meanwhile, the heavy rain fell on the other side of the window. It was as if the rain were accompanying him, or rather as if it were waiting for him at each step, around each corner, like a gray omen of what he would find at the end of his search for the seed of his failure.

"You wouldn't happen to be a cop?" she asked him in turn.

"I'm not a cop, I'm a failure," Samuel said, and once again the woman stared very hard at him, as if she were concentrating on wearing away the contours of his face.

"You're a fraud, that's what you are," she said suddenly.

How was it possible for this woman to call him that? A fraud she'd called him! As if his failure were fraudulent, as if all that anguish over *The Raft of the Medusa* were fraudulent, the whole sordid affair . . . Scandalized, Samuel paid for the coffee, picked up his notebook and left, but before slamming the door shut, he yelled back at the fat barmaid:

"Well you don't look anything like Brad Pitt either!"

And Samuel stepped out into the rain with his gray notebook and he stood there, getting wet; he thought about Sofia, and felt alone. Alone in the rain, by the highway that would carry him to the end of the night and to the end of his own personal failure.

3.

He arrived at Vigo very early in the morning and drove straight to the marina where he knew Armando would be getting ready to set sail. It had stopped raining and a weak white light had set in.

And then he saw her there, on the dock, her hair was longer and the color was different, she was a little thinner and her skin perhaps more tanned, but there was no doubt it was her. He parked his car and walked to where Isolda was busy taking some boxes up to the moored sailboat.

"Hello," he said when he came up beside her. Isolda turned around and her face contorted in an expression of surprise and paled a little.

"Hello Samuel," she answered, trying to recover from her shock, and just then Armando appeared, emerging from the cabin.

"Samuel! Good Lord! What are you doing here? You really have lost your mind . . ."

"Hello Armando. How are you?"

"I can't complain . . . Things haven't been bad to me . . . You know . . . so . . . I see you've already introduced yourself to Isolda," and he continued, addressing himself now to her. "Isolda, this is Samuel. We used to work together. He's a good guy."

Samuel then felt as if reality was trembling in that faint white light. There was the tan face of Isolda, her black eyes and strong features, Armando with his pristine white shirt and his pomaded hair, and that light in which everything was trembling. He looked at his hands, wondering if it was his body that was trembling, but they seemed steady. No, it wasn't him, it was everything else, reality, the world around him, that was trembling. And Samuel saw himself there, as if it was another who was looking, another who he was not. Someone else, free of his failure, was the one now watching as he helped Isolda up the gangplank to the deck, as he followed her, as Armando embraced him and gave him a few slaps on the back, which he felt to be fraudulent. He saw himself talking with them, as if he'd never met Isolda, as if he'd never spent nights beside her, and her playing the role of Armando's perfect lover, a friend of his friend's, and Armando offering them beer, casting off the moorings, and all of them sailing out to sea. Out to sea bathed in a faint white light in which everything trembled. A faint white light exactly the same as the one that lit those wretches in *The Raft of the Medusa*. This disembodied stare continued, and Samuel went on watching himself drink gin and tonics and laughing at Armando's stupid jokes, at Armando, who was getting more and more drunk, at Armando with his eyes glazed over, by now completely blacked out and setting the record straight with Isolda, telling her that he couldn't stand her, that he never should have left his wife for her. Samuel went on watching himself watching Isolda's tears and her telling him, when Armando had gone down to the cabin, that she was sorry, that she was sorry for everything. Everything, absolutely everything. And Samuel's gaze returned to himself and looked out then from his own eyes toward that dark, impenetrable sea into which they were sailing, not toward the germ of his personal failure, he understood, but toward the anguish, hopelessness, and failure of humanity itself, aboard the raft of the Medusa.

The Impostor

PLEASE EXCUSE MY rancid breath, sir. Yes, there we are . . . It's best I talk to you from right here so you won't smell my filth as much. Understand it's been days since I last bathed, and that I'm merely an ailing alcoholic. Sir, I promise to be brief. I don't want to waste your time, but you must understand, I need a little wine and my pockets are all lint. Take pity on a worn-out old man like myself. Let me tell you my story, sir, and if you like it or find it amusing, perhaps you'll give me a few coins, so this poor unfortunate you have before you can get himself a little drink and try to drown his sorrows in alcohol.

Oh, don't look at me like that! I used to be an upstanding man, as I'm sure you are. I understand you, you may rest assured. I know you don't frequent dives like this dark, pestilent hole we're in now, full of losers, alcoholics, and prostitutes. I know, sir, that you aren't like these men or like myself, but I do understand you. I understand that sometimes a respectable, modern man has to let off steam and lose himself in the darkness of seedy dives like this, the darkness of other bodies for a little money, to keep from sinking into his own darkness. Yes, sir! Rest assured, I understand you perfectly, since I was once an upstanding man like yourself.

So please, tell me: Will you let me relate my little tale to you? You don't respond, but I see that slight nod you give me. I can promise that you won't regret having listened, you'll feel freer, the weight of your sorrows light as air, once you've heard about mine, heavy as can be with the weight of the most terrible darkness.

I was once a respectable man like you. Yes, believe me, I know I don't look it now, but I was. Nevertheless, I've always felt the weight of the darkness inside me, the same old horror within me. Yes, sir, the horror! the horror! as Kurtz said, that character of Conrad's from his book in which he told of . . . Oh, but sir! Again, I apologize . . . Excuse my insolence, of course you're already familiar with that book and hardly need me to explain it to you . . . Yes, I felt it within me: the horror. The purest horror. But, you know? there was something that saved me from the horror in those days . . . Yes, but come closer . . . come closer so I can speak in your ear. I know my breath stinks, but I wouldn't want any of these raggedy dead-beats to hear me. Yes, like that. Like that, sir. Now listen: I . . . I used to write stories. Yes, I wrote stories. Every night when I got off work at my miserable job as an accountant, I would go home and take refuge in my small apartment as if it were a miniature fortress protecting me from the outside world, and I'd write. I'd write until I dropped from exhaustion. I'd live other lives, I'd lose myself in other places, I'd look for my own pain in other men in order to evade it. Behind my masks I could dig up my own darkness without its harming me. I could love, kill, die a thousand deaths, and emerge from it all unscathed. I could rape, abuse, and leap into the abyss without falling. I lived and died like this every night, uprooting the pain from my own body and spilling it out onto those blank pages that I'd fill with words, sentences . . . lurking in the darkness of my own heart.

But, you know? that wasn't enough for me; I wanted to go further. Yes, sir, much further than all that. I wanted to take the step from fiction to reality, from literature to the outside world. I wanted to live the life of someone real, not that of a fictitious character, but that of someone who breathed, who could feel pain, love, unhappiness and happiness with his own flesh and soul. So I decided to look for another life, for somebody whose I could take over, so I could lose myself in it, and forget my own. But who? Where was there somebody whose life I could rob and live for myself? And how could it be done?

I meditated on all these setbacks and gradually put that ridiculous idea of the imposture out of my mind. Until one dark night in January when everything changed. At the time I had taken up smoking again, perhaps because I was trying to use cigarettes to calm the anxiety and anguish all those ideas were causing me. On that dark, moonless night, I went down to buy cigarettes. I took the miniscule, rickety elevator to the lobby, and as the door was opening I stepped out and ran literally headfirst into another man who was waiting on the landing. We each got a good blow and then civilly apologized to each other. It was later that night when I began to consider this man.

I was outside shivering on the balcony, smoking a cigarette. I didn't like my small one-room apartment to smell like tobacco. Then a stab of pain in my injured nose reminded me of what had happened only an hour before. Ah yes, the collision getting out of the elevator, that man . . . I thought. But that man . . . What did he look like . . . ? I could produce no picture of him in my mind, no face . . . What kind of face had it been? I wracked my brains trying to remember his features, but it was impossible. I simply couldn't remember his face. Not a single feature. I couldn't remember whether he had a big nose or a small one, whether he wore a beard or was clean-shaven, I couldn't remember his eyes, their color, their cast. Christ! I couldn't even remember whether he was fat or thin, robustly built or a fragile weakling. And I'd been so close to him! We'd smashed into each other with our noses! I couldn't remember whether his breath smelled like mouthwash or was a pestilent, nauseating stench. I couldn't remember his hair. Brown or blond? Maybe he was bald? But wait a minute . . . his hair . . . I couldn't have seen his hair, because he was wearing a hat. Yes, that was it—an old-fashioned hat with a short brim. But who the hell in current-day Barcelona would wear a hat from the thirties or forties?

And with that, sir, began my search for the man in the hat with whom I'd so violently smashed noses. I took note of any man wearing a hat: young, old, fat or thin, haughty or humble. And you wouldn't believe how many people were parading around with that relic on their heads! It was quite the surprise, and I stumbled as well upon the discovery that the short-brimmed hat knew nothing of social classes, and the same one covered the haughty head of some Barcelonan haute-bourgeois out for a stroll around Gracia, as that of some wretch who, with his hat pulled down over his ears, sitting in a doorway, stuck his trembling hand out in my path, begging for a few coins. And in the second case, if I was walking in the daytime along a busy street, I simply gave him a look of disdain and superiority and sped up my pace to put some distance between us; but if the filthy leper dared to stick his dirty hand out at me in a dark street, in the impunity of the night, I would kick him until I stained my boots. And I'm sure you see, sir, the irony of fate: now I'm one of those deadbeat alcoholics, begging you for a few coins; but understand, I was once like you, I was a respectable, modern man who, like any respectable, modern man, hated those who have nothing, who are nothing.

I found him one day at last. Yes, I finally found the man in the hat and, would you believe it, sir, I found him just as I was leaving home one morning. As I was opening the door of my apartment, my neighbor's door across the hall opened at almost exactly the same time, and a man walked out holding a hat, which he immediately put on his head in a smooth, thoughtless way that only comes from long habit. And it was him! The man in the hat was my sixth-floor neighbor! I was speechless. How had I never seen him before? I had lived in that building for five years and that was the first time I'd noticed I had a neighbor. But how? As I was pondering these matters, still frozen with shock, the man politely wished me a good morning. I had the impression the man had said this without moving his lips, but

in my perplexed state I could have been seeing things. Then
he looked at the door of the small elevator and, as if thinking
better of it, spun on his heel and headed off down the stairs,
vanishing like a ghostly figure.

His name was Alberto Queiroz and I found out all I could
about him. He was an insignificant man. Yes, an absolutely
insignificant man, ordinary through and through, without a
shred of personality. He was neither thin nor fat, neither tall
nor short, and I'd be unable to call him either ugly or attractive.
His face was as run-of-the-mill and average as it gets. He was a
ghost who moved among the living without anyone's noticing
his presence. Let me tell you, sir, an utterly insignificant fellow.
The only thing that made him stand apart was the fact that he
wore a hat. That was it. Without his hat he was nobody, he
didn't exist, he was just some light, fleeting thing leaving a faint
wake of oblivion on reality.

I spied on Alberto Queiroz for a while. I would wait behind
my door peering through the peephole at the one across the
hall, behind which he lived. Then I would discreetly follow him
through the city. I stopped going to work in order to do this. I
ate, I slept . . . I lived behind the peephole waiting for Alberto
Queiroz to leave his apartment so I could follow him. He
always did the same thing: he would leave his apartment, close
the door behind him, then look back and forth at the small
elevator and the stairs, as if hesitating, and yet he always ended
up turning abruptly to go down the stairs. This stupid game of
acting as if he were unsure, when he knew full well he was going
to take the stairs, drove me absolutely crazy. Everything always
happened just the way I'm telling you, sir. There was only one
night when the routine ever changed. One single night, when I
was spying on him as usual from behind the peephole, Alberto
Queiroz left his apartment and, as always, paused between the
stairs and the elevator, looking back and forth at one and the
other, but then . . . then he went over and pushed the button

to call the elevator, planting himself squarely in front of it, waiting. I couldn't contain myself and suddenly flung open my door, shouting:

"What are you doing, Mr. Queiroz!"

I immediately realized the mistake of my outburst and how bizarre my words must have sounded. He stared back at me very seriously and said, I could have sworn without parting his lips:

"First of all: good evening, sir; and secondly: I'm going down to buy cigarettes."

I was petrified, and felt so nervous and ridiculous that all I could think of to say was:

"Good, Mr. Queiroz, well, be careful of the dark!" And no sooner had I said this than I felt how doubly ridiculous and senseless these words were, and I slammed the door shut.

That's how my days were spent back then, sir. I knew all about Alberto Queiroz. Every night I would follow him on his strange solitary wanderings around Barcelona. I would follow the faint wake of oblivion that he left in his path, and I must be frank and tell you that I was only able to keep track of him thanks to his short-brimmed hat, without which it would have been impossible not to lose sight of that insignificant, ordinary man who, chameleon-like, would melt into the general ordinariness of the people of Barcelona. In the course of my spying on him, I was led a few nights a month to the strange building where he went for his job, which actually was quite peculiar. It turned out Alberto Queiroz was a ventriloquist! I could now understand why it sometimes seemed he was talking to me without even twitching a lip. And believe you me, sir! He wasn't just any ventriloquist! To start with, the place where he performed was quite strange in itself, it was in a building at the end of a dark alley in the Barrio Gótico. A place called The Other Side. Upon entering I found out why: it was without doubt an homage to Alfred Kubin, the illustrator and writer, because not only was it named after his only novel, but the walls were covered in his gloomy and hallucinatory illustrations. The audience in attendance at these late-night performances was peculiar, too, because they weren't young people hoping to spend a night out on the town, partying and enjoying themselves, but a crowd of all ages who remained in sepulchral silence as Alberto Queiroz appeared on stage. And that, sir, was when the terrific transformation occurred: this ordinary, insignificant man brought his puppets to life, and they weren't your typical, ordinary fare in the least, these beings controlled by Queiroz, coming to life with some voice formed in the pit of his stomach. The people who spoke here were such figures as Camus' Mr. Mersault, reflecting on the absurd and on passivity in the face of the world; or Ferdinan Bardamu of Céline's *Journey to the End of the Night*, who gave a terrific monologue concerning disgust and brutality; Conrad's Captain Marlow hacked his way into a darkness without return, which proved to be that of his own heart; and the protagonist of *The Other Side* by Kubin himself plunged toward the last days of that fantastic realm dominated by collective neurosis, sleeping epidemics, orgies, suicides, and prophets proclaiming the most horrific of all ends.

Yes sir, that's how things were, just as I've said. I spent my days spying on Queiroz, tailing that insignificant man on his nightly walks and slipping into the last row at each of his singular performances at The Other Side, where every time I would witness this ordinary man transforming into his puppets, bringing to life bizarre, original beings. One particular night, I even think he saw me there, at the back of the room. It was toward the end of one of his performances. At the time, he was bringing to life a puppet in the role of the sick, decrepit Russian boy from *Heart of Darkness*, which was conversing with the puppet of Captain Marlow in his search for Kurtz:

"We talked of everything," said the puppet of the young Russian, quite transported at the recollection. "I forgot there was such a thing as sleep. The night did not seem to last an hour. Everything! Everything! . . . Of love, too."

"Ah, he talked to you of love!" Marlow said, much amused.

"It isn't what you think," cried the Russian, almost passionately. "It was in general. He made me see things—things."

Then all the lights in The Other Side went out. Amid the darkness, which was total, a spotlight—a single spotlight—shone on Queiroz. His eyes seemed to be fixed on some point far more distant than the building's rear wall. His shoulders slumped forward as though he'd been suddenly drained by an overwhelming fatigue; the puppets of Marlow and the young Russian drooped lifelessly from his hands. Then Queiroz spoke, but he spoke, once again, without moving his lips, following Conrad's text:

"I looked around, and I don't know why, but I assure you that never, never before, did this land, this river, this jungle, the very arch of this blazing sky, appear to me so hopeless and so dark, so impenetrable to human thought, so pitiless to human weakness."

Then the spotlight illuminating him shut off. A murmur ran through the room, once more in pitch black. Everyone fell silent as another spotlight—smaller this time—lit up only his face. And I swear, sir . . . I swear, Queiroz was staring at me, at my eyes, boring straight into them with his own, and once again, without a single quiver of his lips, a thundering voice emitted from his stomach:

"Be careful of the dark, sir!" he yelled, glaring dourly at me. I ran out of the place in terror, covering the Barrio Gótico as fast as my legs could take me. And when I reached my apartment, I shut myself up inside, taking refuge behind the locked door in a state of total panic.

It went on like this for days. And at the same time as I was spying on Queiroz, I was transforming my own existence into something different from what it had been up to that point, and which was becoming increasingly more like that of Alberto Queiroz, that insignificant man. I dressed like him, imitated his gestures, the way he walked, I even bought a short-brimmed hat like his. I bought all the books, treatises, and miscellaneous writings on ventriloquism I could lay my hands on. I moved the mirror from the bedroom to the small entrance hall by the door, and spent hours watching my own reflection and practicing the art of speaking from the stomach, listening all the while for any movement in the doorway of my neighbor across the hall.

There was only one important matter left to be settled. Something that was indispensable to my plans, but which I didn't quite know how to accomplish. One Tuesday night I armed myself with resolve and mustered up the strength to do it, to get rid of this nagging inconvenience. I waited patiently, going over one of Queiroz's monologues in front of the mirror. Then I heard the sound of the door across the hall being opened. I looked through the peephole. Queiroz was leaving his apartment. He stopped as always to go through his farcical wavering routine in front of the elevator. I was ready and determined. The second Queiroz spun around I opened my door and leaped on him, who had his back to me and was about to head downstairs. I gave him a hard shove. The sight of him trying to regain his foregone balance was comical; he was already soaring irreversibly toward the steps. He fell with a loud thud and rolled down to the fourth-floor landing. I went down after him. Lying there on the ground, he looked like one of his puppets at the end of the show when they hung lifelessly from his hands. He moved slowly, sitting up with great effort, as if he were very tired, and not just like something physical, but like a vital weariness. When he had at last regained his feet, he looked at me. He noticed the taste of blood and touched his face. He took out a white handkerchief, impeccably folded, from his waistcoat pocket, and wiped up the blood from his nose and mouth. I put my right hand into my jacket pocket and, feeling the knife I was carrying there, got ready to put an end to the whole affair. He spoke to me, then, not from his stomach this time, but with his lips:

"Excuse me, sir, I believe I've foolishly tripped and taken a tumble down the stairs. Perhaps they were mopped recently, and are still slippery, although they look dirty enough from here. I'm sorry, sir, but I'm a bit addled, from having struck my head, perhaps. Could you show me where I live? Do you know me?"

"I've never seen you before in my life," I told Queiroz. "And it's really quite bizarre, your being in this building. You see, I live here, and I'm afraid you don't, of course, because otherwise we surely would have met."

"Forgive me, then, please forgive me . . . I just can't seem to remember anything. The fall . . ."

Queiroz looked truly confused. It seemed that he'd lost his memory.

"There's no need to apologize," I said. "We all get a bit dazed and confused sometimes . . . Not to mention that haphazard trip down the stairs you just took . . . But don't worry, you'll see, at any moment your memories will come flooding back and this will all be a funny anecdote you'll tell to your children and your lovely wife. Because I'm sure you have a lovely wife. You have that look about you, and of having some beautiful children, maybe a boy and a girl, the perfect little pair. And . . . you and your friends at the bank will have a good laugh when you tell them about this. Because you have that look about you, of working at a big bank or maybe running some major corporation. Ah, well . . . I'll tell you what . . . You should head downtown, to Las Ramblas. There are plenty of people down that way, and some of those artists sitting on the benches there aren't merely honing their craft, some of them are also collectors . . . collectors of faces, of people . . . I'm sure one of them will recognize you. By the way, even though you obviously can't introduce yourself, I suppose I can: my name's Alberto Queiroz, I'm a ventriloquist."

The man who had once been Alberto Queiroz stared vacantly at me, or through me, rather, into a place that couldn't be seen, and which was all nothingness. Unmitigated absence. He shook my hand. He brushed some dust from his pants and the elbows of his jacket. Then he turned and set off with a slight limp on the slow descent downstairs. I accompanied him to the front door of the building. From there I observed him trudging heavily away into the pitch black of a moonless night, fading from sight toward the end of that unlit alley of the Barrio Gótico. Just at its end, before rounding the corner and vanishing from view, he turned and looked back at me for an instant, as if with some vague impression, as if some doubt were pestering him, the doubt of leaving something behind, something important. An inkling of loss, almost. Before he turned away again and disappeared around the corner, I had time to shout to him:

"Be careful of the dark, sir!"

Ha, ha, ha, ha! See, sir! Quite the madcap tale! Are you having a good time, finding it entertaining? It seems a bit crazy, a bit tall maybe . . . But it's true, I swear! Ha, ha, ha! Now I'm Alberto Queiroz! The living, breathing Queiroz himself! Ha, ha, ha, ha! Oh, sir! But it doesn't end there, no. Of course not. Everything up to this point was so fun, wasn't it? So wild, so fantastic . . . But, you know . . . And I'm sorry if my tone changes as I'm telling you about the rest; I don't mean to get gloomy, I just can't help it. I'm sure you'll understand, you of all people—far better than anybody, perhaps. Besides, there are a few things in what I have left to say which concern you, too, impossible as that may be to believe, yet fate is capricious from time to time, and quite capable of linking up the paths of people so different as, at this juncture, you and I.

Because at this point, sir, I took over Alberto Queiroz's life, leaving my own behind. I transformed myself into a man who was apparently insignificant but who was really a prophet of the stomach. Like the Greek Eurycles of Athens, or Louis Brabant, or Arthur Prince, who could simultaneously speak and drink, and was buried with his wife and his puppet; like Edgar Bergen, whose daughter Candice was jealous of his puppet, with which she had to share a bedroom as if it were her brother, one in each bed, and fall asleep every night gazing over at the inanimate face that gaped up at the ceiling like a corpse.

And so my life of imposture went by, this new life I had elected for myself. I moved into the apartment where the man once known as Alberto Queiroz had lived. I would spill out my "horror" during my shows at The Other Side. I would air out my essential darkness in those monologues, those conversations of my puppets. They didn't talk, it was I. I spoke through their mouths—from my stomach—what I couldn't say. All that seethed in me. All those things . . . those things . . . Until the day I got a phone call that changed everything. It was just starting to get dark outside. I was in front of the mirror preparing for my next performance when the phone rang:

"Hello?" I heard a man's voice say.

"Who is this?" I asked.

"Can you hear me?" said the voice.

"Loud and clear," I said. "Can you hear me?"

"I apologize for calling so late. I'm calling from the Sant Joan clinic. Are you Alberto Queiroz?" said a deliberate, husky voice from the other end of the line.

"Yes, I am. I'm Queiroz," I went along.

"Yes, Mr. Queiroz . . . I should have called you earlier," he said. "We've just now recovered the test results, finally. We've taken quite a while! But you know . . . the fire . . . all that fire . . . What a disaster!"

"Fire? What fire are you talking about?" I asked in surprise—I didn't remember there being any fire in Barcelona recently.

"Yes, the fire . . ." was his only response, and then he went silent, as if he were thinking. "The fire," he resumed, "it destroyed everything. Absolutely everything! Believe me . . . It was an inferno, a real inferno! Hardly any of the medical reports were salvaged. But you're in luck . . ." and he fell silent again, as if he were thinking of the words he'd just said. "Well . . . what I called about was, the results for the tests we ran for you a month ago were some of the only ones we managed to rescue from all the rubble the fire left behind."

"The results? Tests? What the hell are you talking about?" I asked.

The voice then became much huskier.

"You have stomach cancer, Mr. Queiroz," it said.

"But that's impossible . . . It's impossible! . . . You hear me? I'm not Queiroz!" I shouted into the phone.

"Calm down, Mr. Queiroz!" said the voice, huskier still. "You are Alberto Queiroz. Of course you are. I understand, I understand completely," the voice said, and again with each breath it grew huskier, as if some terrible despair had got the better of it. "I understand why you'd want to deny all this. I understand why you'd want to be another person right now and not who you really are. You only have a few months to live. The cancer has already spread too far and to do anything at all would be useless."

"No! You don't understand a damn thing! I . . . I'm not Queiroz . . . I'm . . . I'm . . ." I managed to stutter, and then burst into tears.

"You're Queiroz! And within a few months you'll be dead . . . You won't be anyone anymore. For God's sake, stop crying like a little girl! Spiraling off into chaos will only make things worse, you'll be paralyzed with fear and there won't be any time left for you, there won't be anything left for you. Now you have a few months to live . . . Live them! Don't die in life! Don't let yourself be trapped by the darkness . . . Be careful of the dark,

Mr. Queiroz!" said the voice, which had grown energetic despite
its mounting huskiness, and then, with a clanging slam, the
caller hung up.

Be careful of the dark! Ha, ha, ha . . . ! Be careful of the dark! Ha,
ha, ha, ha . . . ! Everyone repeats the same thing to me over and
over again! That damned meaningless phrase . . . That moronic
phrase I blurted out to Queiroz! Be careful of . . . ! But, sir, how
can you be careful of darkness? Do you know how to be careful
of something like that? How? Dear God! And as you see, sir,
here you have me now, drifting around aimlessly, sick and alcoholic, sludging through the foulest mud of human existence,
in the utterest darkness. She trapped me, I couldn't resist. You
know . . . ? Sir . . . the dark is a woman . . . she calls me on in a
sensual voice. I simply gave in, I just surrendered. And now she
tortures me every night with her subhuman howls, and won't let
me sleep . . . I can't sleep! Do you understand what that's like?
Can you understand, sir? I just drink . . . I drink to deaden my
senses, to muffle her hair-raising screams at night, to hasten the
arrival of my approaching death. To escape the horror! . . . But
sir, could it be that you don't understand me? Yes . . . of course
you do. Maybe someone else wouldn't, but you do . . . you in
particular. So . . . now, sir . . . Why do you look at me like that?
Perhaps my story has made you remember something. Yes . . .
that must be it, or else . . . Is it that you haven't enjoyed my
story . . . ? Oh! Of course you have . . . of course an upstanding, modern man like yourself will now give me a few coins.
Right . . . ? Isn't that right, Mr. Queiroz?

The Italian Letter

DEAR BRUNO, YOU'VE gone too far this time. You've crossed the line. You've taken a step beyond. Until now I allowed you everything, but this is really too much. This, Bruno, I've no intention to allow.

I'll remind you that Olga is my wife, I'll remind you of this because it sometimes seems as though you may have forgotten. Olga has been my wife for twenty years. Twenty years together. Living, with here and there a fleeting sorrow or a joy, but above all living . . . caring for and putting up with each other. You came into our lives just three years ago. Three years in which we have played your game. Three years in which you believe that we have played your game. You have thought of yourself as the one who was directing everything, the one who manipulated the situation at your whim. Olga, on the other hand, believes that it's the both of you, that you do all this for the both of you. For you two and your love, and that it's I whom you and she manipulate like a marionette in your capricious games. So far, I have let it all slide, but this, Bruno, this new maneuver of yours I cannot allow.

When it all began I wanted to kill you, and then I wanted to kill myself. But as you can see, here we are, you, Olga, and I, three years later. All quite alive. I remember when we met you in Milan, this same city where I'm now writing you from. This city, which is your own, so full of you, and in part now also of me. Because, Bruno, as you must know, Olga and I arrived yesterday in Milan, this city I swore I'd never come back to. This cursed city where it all started and where it's all now going to end. This city that's a part of me, the city that bent my life. My predictable life as an organized and realistic man, a deliberate, calm person, who now sees his rectitude bent along a more than uncertain course.

We are in Milan, as you asked Olga in your letter: "On Sunday the fourteenth of August you are to be in Milan, and you'll do it there." You are bold Bruno, you've already demonstrated that to me many times, but this time your boldness runs to stupidity. You have risked too much in your game, you've put up everything. Gone the whole hog. Laid it all down. There's nothing held on to. Nothing left, not even a crumb.

Olga is in the hotel, or perhaps she is praying in some corner of Il Duomo, underneath its marble copulas even I might believe in God, or perhaps she is looking for you, or has already found you and is with you now. I am writing in that café on Via Montenapoleone. You remember it? Yes, it's the same café: the same wrought iron and marble tables, the same wood floors, the same sepia photographs on the wall. Here I am now, Bruno, in your city, which is also partly my own. In the sub-city under the city, in the Milan inside of Milan itself. In the city of narrow streets lined with humble shops and small cafés, which lead into the great avenues full of luxurious window displays, the grand puffed-up boulevards, swollen with their own luxury and grandeur, full, packed, but so empty at the same time. Here I am, under the city's exoskeleton, under the Piazza del Duomo, under the Galleria Vittorio Emanuele II, under Via Manzoni, under the Piazza della Scala, under this very same Via Montenapoleone where I find myself. In this sub-world of narrow streets, miserable cafés, people of indefinite age, impeccably dressed rejects, artists of tightrope walking, poverty and hunger.

I remember how it all began, in this very café. When we were introduced and then left alone, you, Olga, and I. I remember how we talked about literature, about life. Because at bottom

life is no more than what's written. It's no more than the vision
we have of it after reflection, manifest on a sheet of paper. The
rest doesn't exist, there is nothing, not even ourselves, who can
only hope to exist after thought. Then, when it was just the
three of us, you spoke those words of Cesare Pavese's, despicably
passing them off as your own. And although I recognized them
immediately, I didn't say anything, dear Bruno, because that
night, like Olga, I was already in love with you.

"One does not kill himself for love of a woman," you said.
"One kills himself because a love, any love, reveals us in our
nakedness, our misery, our defenselessness, nothingness."

You also spoke to us of Bolaño and his savage detectives, you
spoke to us of visceralism and the lack of visceralism. You told us
that you yourself were a savage explorer, exploring the darkness,
the benighted part of yourself, exploring the Dantesque figures
that writhed in dark corners. You talked to us about your writing
and your poems, so visceral they were nearly pornographic, but
at bottom, I now understand, just as miserable as yourself.

I remember the way Olga looked at you. I knew from the
very first instant. I could see that she'd fallen in love with you
right away, that night when it all began. And I understood her
to a tee, because I, too, fell in love with you that night.

Then came those uncertain and tempestuous days in Milan.
The days of our meetings and mix-ups. The nights in cafés, the
tertulias, the walks through this city's gloomiest corners, the
journeys to the end of the night, as you said, to the unfathomable
depths of our own selves. The nights of alcohol and bohemia
we would cap off in your apartment on Brera or in our hotel
room, where we drunkenly recited poems and fell exhausted to
sleep. The night when you made love to Olga beside me, while
I pretended to be asleep. The night I went to look for you at
your place on Brera in order to kill you, the night I pounded at
your door, hurled insults at you, and we ended up in a tearful
embrace. I cried for us—for you, for Olga, and for me. But I

now know that you, on the other hand, cried only for yourself: for the abyss at your feet, for your vertigo at looking down into the putrid abyss like a cesspit beneath Milan, a bottomless sewer, piled high with corpses whose disfigured faces looked up at you and gradually grew to resemble our own—yours, Olga's, and mine.

When we fled back to Barcelona, we knew that our flight would be impossible, since it's impossible to flee from oneself. But we were fleeing you too, dear Bruno, we fled so we wouldn't kill you, or kill ourselves. Both Olga and I are calm and timid people, and it's because of this I didn't kill you, because, as your admired Pavese said: a suicide is no more than a timid murderer. So we fled from you, and in a certain sense we were trying to kill ourselves after all, or at least kill that thing which had been writhing inside of us ever since that first night when we met in this café, when you slipped it into our lives of quiet sorrows and fleeting joys.

Bruno, why did you have to send that letter? Why? Ever since that moment all of us were doomed, condemned to play that macabre game you devised for us. You addressed that letter to Olga three months after our fleeing from you, perfectly aware that it was I who picked up the mail from our PO Box in Barcelona. I remember vividly the words of the postal clerk when I asked for the mail from my box:

"It looks like you have an Italian letter, sir!" he said with some surprise, as if it were a kind of minor miracle that I had received something not from Barcelona, Madrid, or Valencia.

An Italian letter. You can picture my face when I heard that. The words seemed so out of place there, in Barcelona, where your existence was like something unreal. Nor was I the only one who heard the postal clerk's exclamation—that creature you had polluted me with pricked up its ears as well, nearly dead as it was by then from inanition, from denying your existence. Those words were nourishment for the creature, which began to stir again inside of me, like in Milan, back when I wanted to kill both you and myself, back when you'd embraced me, cried on my shoulder, and petted my face.

That letter was the first of many. They were always addressed to Olga and invariably picked up from the post office by myself. I would read them in my office and then, resealing them with care, hand them over to Olga at night when I arrived home, as if I hadn't read them. Of course, Olga knew I had, and with what great care.

I agreed to play your game. At first I agreed out of love for you, and in part out of love for Olga, too. And once I had agreed that first time, I didn't know how to stop. We agreed to play your morbid game, your stupid game of a frustrated writer.

You started writing the life of Olga, my wife, and therefore mine as well. You would write long letters relating the upcoming days in Olga's life. What she was going to do, how she was going to dress from one day to the next, where she was going to walk in the evenings . . . You would write out what she was going to cook. You would write how she would greet me when I got home, with a kiss, and what kind. You wrote what she was to read, what she was to say to me. At what times she should touch me. How she'd cuddle up to me in bed, how she'd caress me. You transformed Olga into a character from one of your books that you would manipulate at your whim, and you did so to me as well, because I agreed to play the game.

I anxiously awaited your letters, and greedily I read them. And then I awaited Olga's actions. In your words I would read everything my wife would do, the clothes she'd wear, her most intimate thoughts, how she'd greet me when I arrived home. I read of how when night fell she was to slip her fingers under the sheets, in what manner she'd stroke my body, my face, my stomach . . . And from time to time, from my office or some café, I've written you back, as you asked me to, to check up on Olga's actions, just as I'm writing you now, dear Bruno, from

the same old café on Via Montenapoleone, which brings back
so many memories of you.

But Bruno, what you are asking of Olga this time I will not
allow. No Bruno, not this. You've gone too far.

2.

Dear Bruno, I spoke to Olga about you yesterday. It was the
first time in a long while that I had mentioned your name in
her presence. We tried speaking calmly about you. You know
that Olga and I are both timid people, with lives full of quiet
sorrows and fleeting joys. We tried talking rationally about you,
without losing our composure, but in the end it proved impossible and Olga and I wound up in each other's arms, crying
and consoling each other. I spent the remainder of the evening,
until dusk, rereading your manuscripts. I read all of your poems
and stories, while Olga, who had ordered some bottles of wine
from the front desk, remained lying in bed drinking one glass
after another . . . At times I read aloud so she could hear some
fragments from your texts I considered relevant. In all those lines
you wrote in the end I have wound up meeting with my own
self. Encountering in other recesses the same void. The same
void which, like a silent nocturnal bird, alights beside me, turns
its gray lifeless eyes on mine, and in my own voice tells me, I
am the same.

Now in the dark of night I felt confused. Doubts threatened
me. Doubts about you, Bruno. I considered that perhaps your
macabre game would end with one big closing joke. You had,
perhaps, one great last joke to bring this stupid game of letters
to an end. Would this big last laugh be your non-existence,
was it all a farce? Perhaps it was this twisted end you had in
store for us, and then the game you dreamt up would be over.
But if so, Bruno, then who are you? Are you merely one of my

inventions? Is it possible the three of us never met in that café on Via Montenapoleone? Might it have been I who spoke those words of Cesare Pavese, passing them off as my own? Was it I who got drunk and recited poetry out loud until I dropped from exhaustion? Was I the one who made love to Olga that night in Milan imagining it was you doing so, imagining myself watching you two while I pretended to be sleeping? And for that matter, am I the one who wrote these texts? Am I the author of these poems, of these stories now scattered across the floor? Is your vertigo, Bruno, my vertigo?

And what about the letters? All those letters. Did I send them myself? Was it I who, from my office, wrote those letters, signing your name to them, putting down for the return address an imaginary place in Milan and mailing them to my own post-office box? Am I the ultimate author of this twisted game in which Olga has agreed to participate?

I'm now sitting in this café, our café, on Via Montenapoleone. The café where I met you or imagined I met you. Night is falling on Milan, which fights back against the darkness, gleams, lights up in all its false splendor, its empty, golden splendor. But there are still dark corners where no light whatsoever can penetrate. The corners where your characters have their existence, Bruno, where those beings who swarm through your manuscripts live, love, perspire, and feed. Those beings who, as Kafka said, eat the scraps from their own table, because that way they are satisfied a little longer than the rest, but who forget how to eat from the table, with which the scraps, too, cease. Those beings like you, like Olga, like myself.

So here I am, sitting in this café surrounded by darkness, surrounded by shadows moving with impunity in the blackness, writhing, swinging their hips, whoring themselves, selling their bodies, their souls, their own children. So here I am, sitting in this wooden chair, with my elbows leaning on the table on which rests the letter I'm writing you. Looking at the window where I can see my own reflection—my face watching me from the glass.

And, finally, I understand.

It's all clear to me now.

Here you are Bruno. My beloved Bruno. How could I have doubted you? How could I have been capable of questioning your existence? Bruno, my Bruno . . . I can see you now, watching me. Watching me from my image reflected in the glass. Watching me from the reflection of my eyes, from the darkness of Milan, from our darkness.

At last, I understand you. It took only your looking into my eyes this way for me to understand. For me to grasp your intentions. For me to comprehend the meaning of your proposal. And . . . how can I say no? How can I deny you now? Now that with this look all's been explained, with no further need of words. Now Bruno, my beloved Bruno, I will do what you ask.

Under Water

1.

THE HIGHWAY WINDS through fields and industrial zones. I'm in another country or another region unfamiliar to me in a pitch-dark night, under a pouring rain. I have been driving on secondary roads for several hours and I'm now approaching the big city, but the highway is no better, there are just more cars, creeping along very slowly. You can't see more than six feet ahead in the rain. I listen to the monotonous sound of the windshield wipers and the raindrops on the glass. The traffic comes to a halt. I look outside, toward the shoulder of the highway, barely able to make out anything at all in the impenetrable darkness. We move ahead a few more yards and stop again as the rain appears to be growing worse, and then, knock, knock, someone raps against the window. I look: there's a woman outside. I peer through the rain to try and get a better look: I notice she's dressed up like a prostitute and lock the door. We move ahead a few more yards, but the woman, soaked to the skin, follows alongside the car and taps again on the glass. I decide to unlock the door and she opens it and gets inside. Her soaked clothes and hair stick to her body. She takes off her high heels, says something to me in a foreign language, which I don't understand, and then sits there in silence.

I, on the other hand, start to talk, after a while. As if I were delivering an internal monologue out loud—since I'm perfectly aware she won't understand my language—I start to relate what happened to me a few hours ago, as we advance yard by yard toward the big city.

"Before I got to this highway, I traveled a long time on other ones, local ones I didn't know. As dusk was falling, I pulled over by some farmland that looked half-abandoned. The evening breeze was whispering in the leaves of the poplars swaying gently under the gray sky. I got out of the car, lit a cigarette, and looked out over the fields disappearing into the horizon. The farm plots were separated from each other by low, crumbling cobblestone walls, and there were small copses scattered here and there. I had absurdly stopped to smoke a cigarette, even knowing that I was running late for wherever it was I had to go. Time was sneaking up on me on this winding, unfamiliar, and lightless highway, and I wondered how I was going to find the main highway if night fell. But it was only a thought, and instead of continuing on my way, I went down a path leading into the barren plots.

"When I had gone some hundred yards I saw it. Its fur was short and black, its back flecked with some patches of ochre, and it was running toward me at full speed. The dog looked rabid. When it came to where I was standing, it ran around me barking, as if it was possessed. It barked into the dusk at nobody, as if defending itself from an imaginary pursuer. It ran around me howling, jumping, and barking. I was scared and tried to kick it away from me, but it got tangled in my legs and I fell. Lying on the parched ground, I could smell the fetid odor coming from the animal's throat and feel the touch of its rough, hardened coat. I managed to get back to my feet and run away from there, with the animal following close at my heels. And when I got to the car and hurriedly closed the door, the dog went on circling the automobile, barking and whining as if something invisible were provoking in it a terrible pain. I started the car, and as I did, I thought I heard someone shouting my name.

"'Antonio!' I thought I heard, and I had the impression that the voice calling me was a woman's. Then, as I put the car in gear and drove away, I heard the terrible scream of the animal under the wheels."

Once I finish telling this anecdote, I don't say anything else until we get to the city. She does not emit any sound either, and there only seem to exist the eternal rain pattering on the glass and the back and forth of the windshield wipers. I take a few turns, disoriented, on poorly lit and unfamiliar streets, until I manage to find the hotel. I park in a spot near the entrance. The woman gets out with me and follows me shivering from cold and soaking wet on her ridiculous high heels. I tell her to go away:

"Go on! Get out of here!" I shout at her, but she doesn't go. So she comes with me into the hotel and at the front desk I ask for a double room.

In the room there's a single, full-size bed. I sit down on it and want to smoke, but when I take the pack out of my pocket I realize that all the cigarettes are wet.

"Shit! Fucking country!" I yell, springing up to my feet.

The woman looks at me.

"Fuck! Your country's a shithole!" I shout at her.

Presently, I manage to calm down and sit back down on the bed. She starts to take off her clothes. She undresses completely and gets into bed behind me. I don't look at her, but I can smell her wet hair. I sense its smell and for some reason I think of the smell of the dog and of its final piercing scream. Thinking of this, I become very sad. I think of unpleasant things: wives dying of cancer, all those things I think of sometimes.

"I was that dog," comes her voice from behind me in perfect Spanish.

I stay silent. I breathe and count to ten. Then I turn around. There is a dead dog lying in my bed.

2.

There are places that are fictitious but that are real to oneself. Or maybe it's only that reality's been distorted to the point where one city turns into another. By your way of looking at it, your nostalgia for what's lost, or even the nostalgia for feeling nostalgia for something, the void that's left when even your pain has left you, and you realize you don't feel anything, and that there's no longer anything or anyone to look forward to. Oporto stretches out below me. I look down at it from the large window of my hotel room. It's not really Oporto—not the city, the people, the light, the shades of glazed tilework that's falling to pieces. No, it's another city slowly awakening at my feet—breathing, sweating, writhing, shedding its skin every hour in this feeble light in which things are not exactly things.

"There was a period after you left when I had this same feeling," I say, turning to face her. "All around there was this same irreality, the same murkiness in things. Everything seemed slippery, like now . . . Goddamn it . . . ! You shouldn't have left me like that . . ."

"Do you think I didn't struggle?" she says.

The light seems liquid, it's as if I were looking at things . . . under water . . . Yes, that's it—I think—it's as if I'm looking at things through water. The light distorts the shapes of things, their distance from me. I pick up the jacket spread over the back of the chair, I carefully fold it.

"Look . . . This is what I have left: the things that were, this jacket, the small habits I picked up living with you, even the same pen you gave me once, I refill it with ink over and over—"

"Antonio," she cuts in. "Aren't you going to leave me alone? Why are you doing this?"

"Because I'm afraid."

"Antonio, I'm dead."

I unfold the jacket, put it on, and walk to the door, turning my back on her. I place my hand on the doorknob. To open the door and leave, that's all I want. I focus on what for most people are simple motions: turning the knob, opening the door, stepping out of the room, and closing the door behind me without looking back. I do all this, except as I'm leaving I turn around before shutting the door, and from there in the hallway the room looks empty. There isn't any woman, and there isn't any dead dog on the bed either. Gently turning the knob, I close the door, and from the other side I hear her muffled voice:

"Why'd you dress me up like a whore? And why Oporto? We've never been to Oporto. And Portuguese? I can barely say one word . . ."

On the way down to the hotel bar, I check my watch, which confirms that the morning is now wearing on, even though the light remains dim, diluted. I order coffee and take my beat-up notebook from my pocket, and in gradually smaller, nearly illegible handwriting, like that Swiss writer once used, I try to express in words this light's effect on things. And I do this with the old pen she gave me, whose ink I've refilled a thousand times. Then I pay for the coffee and go back up to the room— no one's there.

I sit down on the edge of the bed, pick up the phone from the nightstand and ask room service to send up a large cup of coffee with cream and four packets of sugar. Once it's been delivered, and the diligent bellhop has carefully closed the door behind him, I open the nightstand drawer, take out a pill bottle, and empty the ten remaining capsules on the wooden tabletop. I crack them open, one by one, pouring the dirty-white powder into the coffee, then I open the four sugar packets and pour them in too; I stir well and drink it all down in two swallows.

Then, for some reason, I think of the last sentence of a certain Chekhov story:

And it seemed as though in a little while the solution would be found, and then a new and glorious life would begin; and it was clear to both of them that the end was still far off, and that what was to be most complicated and difficult for them was only just beginning.

And this story's final sentence violently awakens a wave of despair that overwhelms me. I try to calm down: sleep—I think—little by little will numb me and this feeling of anguish will fade away. But it doesn't, it doesn't fade, and the anguish turns to panic, and then I call her. I call her, shouting: Come back! Come back! Please! Come back . . . ! I don't want to die! And I try to reach the phone to call for help, but I can't. It's as if it were hundreds of yards away from me: my arms, my legs don't respond. My body is paralyzed and I feel the dark shadow of sleep falling over me as my eyelids grow heavy and begin to close, but before they shut, I see her hand pick up the phone. I look at her: she looks so nervous and her lower lip trembles as she speaks.

CARLOS MALENO was born on October 4, 1977, in Almería, Spain, where he resides still, having lived for a time in Madrid, where he studied Economics. He works as an international sales broker at a produce company. His most recent novel is *The Endless Rose* (2015).

ERIC KURTZKE was born on April 16, 1990, in Durham, North Carolina. He studied English literature at the University of Notre Dame and currently teaches English in Mexico City.

MICHAL AJVAZ, *The Golden Age.*
The Other City.
PIERRE ALBERT-BIROT, *Grabinoulor.*
YUZ ALESHKOVSKY, *Kangaroo.*
FELIPE ALFAU, *Chromos.*
Locos.
JOE AMATO, *Samuel Taylor's Last Night.*
IVAN ÂNGELO, *The Celebration.*
The Tower of Glass.
ANTÓNIO LOBO ANTUNES, *Knowledge of Hell.*
The Splendor of Portugal.
ALAIN ARIAS-MISSON, *Theatre of Incest.*
JOHN ASHBERY & JAMES SCHUYLER, *A Nest of Ninnies.*
ROBERT ASHLEY, *Perfect Lives.*
GABRIELA AVIGUR-ROTEM, *Heatwave and Crazy Birds.*
DJUNA BARNES, *Ladies Almanack.*
Ryder.
JOHN BARTH, *Letters.*
Sabbatical.
DONALD BARTHELME, *The King.*
Paradise.
SVETISLAV BASARA, *Chinese Letter.*
MIQUEL BAUÇÀ, *The Siege in the Room.*
RENÉ BELLETTO, *Dying.*
MAREK BIENCZYK, *Transparency.*
ANDREI BITOV, *Pushkin House.*
ANDREJ BLATNIK, *You Do Understand.*
Law of Desire.
LOUIS PAUL BOON, *Chapel Road.*
My Little War.
Summer in Termuren.
ROGER BOYLAN, *Killoyle.*
IGNÁCIO DE LOYOLA BRANDÃO, *Anonymous Celebrity.*
Zero.
BONNIE BREMSER, *Troia: Mexican Memoirs.*
CHRISTINE BROOKE-ROSE, *Amalgamemnon.*
BRIGID BROPHY, *In Transit.*
The Prancing Novelist.

GERALD L. BRUNS, *Modern Poetry and the Idea of Language.*
GABRIELLE BURTON, *Heartbreak Hotel.*
MICHEL BUTOR, *Degrees.*
Mobile.
G. CABRERA INFANTE, *Infante's Inferno.*
Three Trapped Tigers.
JULIETA CAMPOS, *The Fear of Losing Eurydice.*
ANNE CARSON, *Eros the Bittersweet.*
ORLY CASTEL-BLOOM, *Dolly City.*
LOUIS-FERDINAND CÉLINE, *North.*
Conversations with Professor Y.
London Bridge.
MARIE CHAIX, *The Laurels of Lake Constance.*
HUGO CHARTERIS, *The Tide Is Right.*
ERIC CHEVILLARD, *Demolishing Nisard.*
The Author and Me.
MARC CHOLODENKO, *Mordechai Schamz.*
JOSHUA COHEN, *Witz.*
EMILY HOLMES COLEMAN, *The Shutter of Snow.*
ERIC CHEVILLARD, *The Author and Me.*
ROBERT COOVER, *A Night at the Movies.*
STANLEY CRAWFORD, *Log of the S.S. The Mrs Unguentine.*
Some Instructions to My Wife.
RENÉ CREVEL, *Putting My Foot in It.*
RALPH CUSACK, *Cadenza.*
NICHOLAS DELBANCO, *Sherbrookes.*
The Count of Concord.
NIGEL DENNIS, *Cards of Identity.*
PETER DIMOCK, *A Short Rhetoric for Leaving the Family.*
ARIEL DORFMAN, *Konfidenz.*
COLEMAN DOWELL, *Island People.*
Too Much Flesh and Jabez.
ARKADII DRAGOMOSHCHENKO, *Dust.*
RIKKI DUCORNET, *Phosphor in Dreamland.*
The Complete Butcher's Tales.

RIKKI DUCORNET (cont.), *The Jade Cabinet*.
The Fountains of Neptune.

WILLIAM EASTLAKE, *The Bamboo Bed*.
Castle Keep.
Lyric of the Circle Heart.

JEAN ECHENOZ, *Chopin's Move*.

STANLEY ELKIN, *A Bad Man*.
Criers and Kibitzers, Kibitzers and Criers.
The Dick Gibson Show.
The Franchiser.
The Living End.
Mrs. Ted Bliss.

FRANÇOIS EMMANUEL, *Invitation to a Voyage*.

PAUL EMOND, *The Dance of a Sham*.

SALVADOR ESPRIU, *Ariadne in the Grotesque Labyrinth*.

LESLIE A. FIEDLER, *Love and Death in the American Novel*.

JUAN FILLOY, *Op Oloop*.

ANDY FITCH, *Pop Poetics*.

GUSTAVE FLAUBERT, *Bouvard and Pécuchet*.

KASS FLEISHER, *Talking out of School*.

JON FOSSE, *Aliss at the Fire*.
Melancholy.

FORD MADOX FORD, *The March of Literature*.

MAX FRISCH, *I'm Not Stiller*.
Man in the Holocene.

CARLOS FUENTES, *Christopher Unborn*.
Distant Relations.
Terra Nostra.
Where the Air Is Clear.

TAKEHIKO FUKUNAGA, *Flowers of Grass*.

WILLIAM GADDIS, JR., *The Recognitions*.

JANICE GALLOWAY, *Foreign Parts*.
The Trick Is to Keep Breathing.

WILLIAM H. GASS, *Life Sentences*.
The Tunnel.
The World Within the Word.
Willie Masters' Lonesome Wife.

GÉRARD GAVARRY, *Hoppla! 1 2 3*.

ETIENNE GILSON, *The Arts of the Beautiful*.
Forms and Substances in the Arts.

C. S. GISCOMBE, *Giscome Road*.
Here.

DOUGLAS GLOVER, *Bad News of the Heart*.

WITOLD GOMBROWICZ, *A Kind of Testament*.

PAULO EMÍLIO SALES GOMES, *P's Three Women*.

GEORGI GOSPODINOV, *Natural Novel*.

JUAN GOYTISOLO, *Count Julian*.
Juan the Landless.
Makbara.
Marks of Identity.

HENRY GREEN, *Blindness*.
Concluding.
Doting.
Nothing.

JACK GREEN, *Fire the Bastards!*

JIŘÍ GRUŠA, *The Questionnaire*.

MELA HARTWIG, *Am I a Redundant Human Being?*

JOHN HAWKES, *The Passion Artist*.
Whistlejacket.

ELIZABETH HEIGHWAY, ED., *Contemporary Georgian Fiction*.

AIDAN HIGGINS, *Balcony of Europe*.
Blind Man's Bluff.
Bornholm Night-Ferry.
Langrishe, Go Down.
Scenes from a Receding Past.

KEIZO HINO, *Isle of Dreams*.

KAZUSHI HOSAKA, *Plainsong*.

ALDOUS HUXLEY, *Antic Hay*.
Point Counter Point.
Those Barren Leaves.
Time Must Have a Stop.

NAOYUKI II, *The Shadow of a Blue Cat*.

DRAGO JANČAR, *The Tree with No Name*.

MIKHEIL JAVAKHISHVILI, *Kvachi*.

GERT JONKE, *The Distant Sound*.
Homage to Czerny.
The System of Vienna.

FOR A FULL LIST OF PUBLICATIONS, VISIT: www.dalkeyarchive.com

JACQUES JOUET, *Mountain R.*
Savage.
Upstaged.

MIEKO KANAI, *The Word Book.*

YORAM KANIUK, *Life on Sandpaper.*

ZURAB KARUMIDZE, *Dagny.*

JOHN KELLY, *From Out of the City.*

HUGH KENNER, *Flaubert, Joyce
and Beckett: The Stoic Comedians.*
Joyce's Voices.

DANILO KIŠ, *The Attic.*
The Lute and the Scars.
Psalm 44.
A Tomb for Boris Davidovich.

ANITA KONKKA, *A Fool's Paradise.*

GEORGE KONRÁD, *The City Builder.*

TADEUSZ KONWICKI, *A Minor
Apocalypse.*
The Polish Complex.

ANNA KORDZAIA-SAMADASHVILI,
Me, Margarita.

MENIS KOUMANDAREAS, *Koula.*

ELAINE KRAF, *The Princess of 72nd Street.*

JIM KRUSOE, *Iceland.*

AYSE KULIN, *Farewell: A Mansion in
Occupied Istanbul.*

EMILIO LASCANO TEGUI, *On Elegance
While Sleeping.*

ERIC LAURRENT, *Do Not Touch.*

VIOLETTE LEDUC, *La Bâtarde.*

EDOUARD LEVÉ, *Autoportrait.*
Newspaper.
Suicide.
Works.

MARIO LEVI, *Istanbul Was a Fairy Tale.*

DEBORAH LEVY, *Billy and Girl.*

JOSÉ LEZAMA LIMA, *Paradiso.*

ROSA LIKSOM, *Dark Paradise.*

OSMAN LINS, *Avalovara.*
The Queen of the Prisons of Greece.

FLORIAN LIPUŠ, *The Errors of Young Tjaž.*

GORDON LISH, *Peru.*

ALF MACLOCHLAINN, *Out of Focus.*
Past Habitual.

The Corpus in the Library.

RON LOEWINSOHN, *Magnetic Field(s).*

YURI LOTMAN, *Non-Memoirs.*

D. KEITH MANO, *Take Five.*

MINA LOY, *Stories and Essays of Mina Loy.*

MICHELINE AHARONIAN MARCOM,
A Brief History of Yes.
The Mirror in the Well.

BEN MARCUS, *The Age of Wire and String.*

WALLACE MARKFIELD, *Teitlebaum's
Window.*

DAVID MARKSON, *Reader's Block.*
Wittgenstein's Mistress.

CAROLE MASO, *AVA.*

HISAKI MATSUURA, *Triangle.*

LADISLAV MATEJKA & KRYSTYNA
POMORSKA, EDS., *Readings in Russian
Poetics: Formalist & Structuralist Views.*

HARRY MATHEWS, *Cigarettes.*
The Conversions.
The Human Country.
The Journalist.
My Life in CIA.
Singular Pleasures.
The Sinking of the Odradek.
Stadium.
Tlooth.

HISAKI MATSUURA, *Triangle.*

DONAL MCLAUGHLIN, *beheading the
virgin mary, and other stories.*

JOSEPH MCELROY, *Night Soul and
Other Stories.*

ABDELWAHAB MEDDEB, *Talismano.*

GERHARD MEIER, *Isle of the Dead.*

HERMAN MELVILLE, *The Confidence-
Man.*

AMANDA MICHALOPOULOU, *I'd Like.*

STEVEN MILLHAUSER, *The Barnum
Museum.*
In the Penny Arcade.

RALPH J. MILLS, JR., *Essays on Poetry.*

MOMUS, *The Book of Jokes.*

CHRISTINE MONTALBETTI, *The Origin
of Man.*
Western.

NICHOLAS MOSLEY, *Accident.*
Assassins.
Catastrophe Practice.
A Garden of Trees.
Hopeful Monsters.
Imago Bird.
Inventing God.
Look at the Dark.
Metamorphosis.
Natalie Natalia.
Serpent.

WARREN MOTTE, *Fables of the Novel: French Fiction since 1990.*
Fiction Now: The French Novel in the 21st Century.
Mirror Gazing.
Oulipo: A Primer of Potential Literature.

GERALD MURNANE, *Barley Patch.*
Inland.

YVES NAVARRE, *Our Share of Time.*
Sweet Tooth.

DOROTHY NELSON, *In Night's City.*
Tar and Feathers.

ESHKOL NEVO, *Homesick.*

WILFRIDO D. NOLLEDO, *But for the Lovers.*

BORIS A. NOVAK, *The Master of Insomnia.*

FLANN O'BRIEN, *At Swim-Two-Birds.*
The Best of Myles.
The Dalkey Archive.
The Hard Life.
The Poor Mouth.
The Third Policeman.

CLAUDE OLLIER, *The Mise-en-Scène.*
Wert and the Life Without End.

PATRIK OUŘEDNÍK, *Europeana.*
The Opportune Moment, 1855.

BORIS PAHOR, *Necropolis.*

FERNANDO DEL PASO, *News from the Empire.*
Palinuro of Mexico.

ROBERT PINGET, *The Inquisitory.*
Mahu or The Material.
Trio.

MANUEL PUIG, *Betrayed by Rita Hayworth.*

The Buenos Aires Affair.
Heartbreak Tango.

RAYMOND QUENEAU, *The Last Days.*
Odile.
Pierrot Mon Ami.
Saint Glinglin.

ANN QUIN, *Berg.*
Passages.
Three.
Tripticks.

ISHMAEL REED, *The Free-Lance Pallbearers.*
The Last Days of Louisiana Red.
Ishmael Reed: The Plays.
Juice!
The Terrible Threes.
The Terrible Twos.
Yellow Back Radio Broke-Down.

JASIA REICHARDT, *15 Journeys Warsaw to London.*

JOÃO UBALDO RIBEIRO, *House of the Fortunate Buddhas.*

JEAN RICARDOU, *Place Names.*

RAINER MARIA RILKE,
The Notebooks of Malte Laurids Brigge.

JULIÁN RÍOS, *The House of Ulysses.*
Larva: A Midsummer Night's Babel.
Poundemonium.

ALAIN ROBBE-GRILLET, *Project for a Revolution in New York.*
A Sentimental Novel.

AUGUSTO ROA BASTOS, *I the Supreme.*

DANIËL ROBBERECHTS, *Arriving in Avignon.*

JEAN ROLIN, *The Explosion of the Radiator Hose.*

OLIVIER ROLIN, *Hotel Crystal.*

ALIX CLEO ROUBAUD, *Alix's Journal.*

JACQUES ROUBAUD, *The Form of a City Changes Faster, Alas, Than the Human Heart.*
The Great Fire of London.
Hortense in Exile.
Hortense Is Abducted.
Mathematics: The Plurality of Worlds of Lewis.
Some Thing Black.

RAYMOND ROUSSEL, *Impressions of Africa.*

VEDRANA RUDAN, *Night.*

PABLO M. RUIZ, *Four Cold Chapters on the Possibility of Literature.*

GERMAN SADULAEV, *The Maya Pill.*

TOMAŽ ŠALAMUN, *Soy Realidad.*

LYDIE SALVAYRE, *The Company of Ghosts.*
The Lecture.
The Power of Flies.

LUIS RAFAEL SÁNCHEZ, *Macho Camacho's Beat.*

SEVERO SARDUY, *Cobra & Maitreya.*

NATHALIE SARRAUTE, *Do You Hear Them?*
Martereau.
The Planetarium.

STIG SÆTERBAKKEN, *Siamese.*
Self-Control.
Through the Night.

ARNO SCHMIDT, *Collected Novellas.*
Collected Stories.
Nobodaddy's Children.
Two Novels.

ASAF SCHURR, *Motti.*

GAIL SCOTT, *My Paris.*

DAMION SEARLS, *What We Were Doing and Where We Were Going.*

JUNE AKERS SEESE, *Is This What Other Women Feel Too?*

BERNARD SHARE, *Inish.*
Transit.

VIKTOR SHKLOVSKY, *Bowstring.*
Literature and Cinematography.
Theory of Prose.
Third Factory.
Zoo, or Letters Not about Love.

PIERRE SINIAC, *The Collaborators.*

KJERSTI A. SKOMSVOLD, *The Faster I Walk, the Smaller I Am.*

JOSEF ŠKVORECKÝ, *The Engineer of Human Souls.*

GILBERT SORRENTINO, *Aberration of Starlight.*
Blue Pastoral.
Crystal Vision.

Imaginative Qualities of Actual Things.
Mulligan Stew. Red the Fiend.
Steelwork.
Under the Shadow.

MARKO SOSIČ, *Ballerina, Ballerina.*

ANDRZEJ STASIUK, *Dukla.*
Fado.

GERTRUDE STEIN, *The Making of Americans.*
A Novel of Thank You.

LARS SVENDSEN, *A Philosophy of Evil.*

PIOTR SZEWC, *Annihilation.*

GONÇALO M. TAVARES, *A Man: Klaus Klump.*
Jerusalem.
Learning to Pray in the Age of Technique.

LUCIAN DAN TEODOROVICI, *Our Circus Presents...*

NIKANOR TERATOLOGEN, *Assisted Living.*

STEFAN THEMERSON, *Hobson's Island.*
The Mystery of the Sardine.
Tom Harris.

TAEKO TOMIOKA, *Building Waves.*

JOHN TOOMEY, *Sleepwalker.*

DUMITRU TSEPENEAG, *Hotel Europa.*
The Necessary Marriage.
Pigeon Post.
Vain Art of the Fugue.

ESTHER TUSQUETS, *Stranded.*

DUBRAVKA UGRESIC, *Lend Me Your Character.*
Thank You for Not Reading.

TOR ULVEN, *Replacement.*

MATI UNT, *Brecht at Night.*
Diary of a Blood Donor.
Things in the Night.

ÁLVARO URIBE & OLIVIA SEARS, EDS., *Best of Contemporary Mexican Fiction.*

ELOY URROZ, *Friction.*
The Obstacles.

LUISA VALENZUELA, *Dark Desires and the Others.*
He Who Searches.

PAUL VERHAEGHEN, *Omega Minor.*

BORIS VIAN, *Heartsnatcher.*

LLORENÇ VILLALONGA, *The Dolls' Room.*

TOOMAS VINT, *An Unending Landscape.*

ORNELA VORPSI, *The Country Where No One Ever Dies.*

AUSTRYN WAINHOUSE, *Hedyphagetica.*

CURTIS WHITE, *America's Magic Mountain.*
The Idea of Home.
Memories of My Father Watching TV.
Requiem.

DIANE WILLIAMS,
Excitability: Selected Stories.
Romancer Erector.

DOUGLAS WOOLF, *Wall to Wall.*
Ya! & John-Juan.

JAY WRIGHT, *Polynomials and Pollen.*
The Presentable Art of Reading Absence.

PHILIP WYLIE, *Generation of Vipers.*

MARGUERITE YOUNG, *Angel in the Forest.*
Miss MacIntosh, My Darling.

REYOUNG, *Unbabbling.*

VLADO ŽABOT, *The Succubus.*

ZORAN ŽIVKOVIĆ, *Hidden Camera.*

LOUIS ZUKOFSKY, *Collected Fiction.*

VITOMIL ZUPAN, *Minuet for Guitar.*

SCOTT ZWIREN, *God Head.*

AND MORE . . .